Tree-Climbing Contest

I spotted a tree I thought would be good. "This is the one I want," I said, hoping it was as good as Jed's.

"Good. Then we're ready," said Sam. "Okay, referees, make sure you note any slips or falls."

"You can fall on me any time you want to, Jed," said Brenda with a disgusting, love-sick smile.

"All right," Sam interrupted. "Let's get this contest going before the counselors find us."

He gave the signal and we were off. I guess I was a bit overeager. I was climbing so quickly I failed to notice a rotten area on a branch I was reaching for. It gave way, and I slipped, just barely managing to keep from falling.

"Slip! Minus one for Linda!" Matt called out.

Darn! I slowed my pace a bit and glanced over at Jed, just in time to see him reach for a branch that was way too small to hold his weight.

"No, Jed, don't!" I warned, but he didn't listen.

Books by Linda Lewis

THE TOMBOY TERROR IN BUNK 109
2 YOUNG
2 GO
4 BOYS
WANT TO TRADE TWO BROTHERS FOR A CAT?

Available from MINSTREL Books

WE HATE EVERYTHING BUT BOYS
IS THERE LIFE AFTER BOYS?
WE LOVE ONLY OLDER BOYS
MY HEART BELONGS TO THAT BOY
ALL FOR THE LOVE OF THAT BOY
DEDICATED TO THAT BOY I LOVE
LOVING TWO IS HARD TO DO

Available from ARCHWAY Paperbacks

THE TOMBOY TERROR IN BUNK 109

Linda Lewis

A MINSTREL® BOOK

PUBLISHED BY POCKET BOOKS

New York   London   Toronto   Sydney   Tokyo   Singapore

A MINSTREL PAPERBACK *ORIGINAL*

 A Minstrel Book published by
POCKET BOOKS, a division of Simon & Schuster
1230 Avenue of the Americas, New York, NY 10020

ISBN 10: 1-416-97539-7
ISBN 13: 978-1-416-97539-7

First Minstrel Books printing June 1991

10 9 8 7 6 5 4 3 2 1

*To my terrific nephews and niece
Brad, Sam, Jed, and Farah*

THE TOMBOY TERROR IN BUNK 109

Chapter
One

It was total confusion. Kids of all ages were coming and going, calling out greetings to their friends, kissing their parents goodbye, and weaving in and out of the crowd as they tried to find where they belonged. The only reason I knew I was in the right place was that the row of buses said Camp Winnepeg on them, as did the big banner stretched across the wall.

I didn't want any part of it. I turned to my mother and made one last effort to get through to her. "Ma, it's still not too late to back out of this. Take me home with you, please. Don't make me go to camp!"

I might as well have been talking to a stone wall. "Now, Linda, don't start that nonsense again," Mom warned, her normally pleasant face distorted by a frown. "Any other child would be grateful for the chance to go away to camp. You'll get out of hot, muggy New York City for three whole weeks in August. You'll enjoy the beauty of nature in the country. You can go swimming and have activities with girls and boys your own age. You'll have a wonderful time!"

"That's what you think," I grumbled. "I'll never have a good time in any camp that has Brenda Roman in it!"

No sooner did I say the dreaded name than Brenda Roman, herself, appeared on the scene. Stuck-up Brenda showed up for camp with her big green and red parrot, Pretty Boy, perched upon her shoulder.

"Pretty Boy, Pretty Boy! Pretty Boy loves Brenda! Pretty Boy loves beautiful Brenda!" the parrot announced. This caused quite a stir among the crowd of campers. Everyone stopped to stare at Brenda and her bird.

"Wow! He's beautiful!" "I can't believe he's real!" "How do you get him to stay on your shoulder?" "Are you taking him to camp?" "How come he doesn't fly away?" Everyone threw comments and questions at Brenda.

She shook her cloud of curly brown hair. You could see that she ate up being the center of attention. Why else would she bring her dumb old bird to the bus station?

"Pretty Boy stays on my shoulder because he loves me so much. Besides, his wings are clipped, of course. And I'm not taking him to camp—he's just here to spend every last minute of time with me he can," she told her admirers.

Brenda was so busy strutting about and showing off her bird that she didn't even look where she was going.

Or maybe she knew exactly where she was going and got me on purpose. At any rate, as she and Pretty Boy passed by where I was standing with my mother, she placed her designer-sneaker clad foot right down on my big toe.

"Ow, my toe! Don't you even look where you're going?" I said, giving her a shove that was a lot more gentle than what she deserved.

"Darn it, Linda, must you always be so rough?" Brenda demanded angrily. Then she caught sight of my mother and changed her tone of voice. "I mean— uh—excuse me. I hope I didn't hurt you! It's just so crowded here with all these newcomers, who don't have any idea of what's going on."

Brenda smiled sweetly when she said this, but I knew what she meant. Brenda had been going to Camp Winnepeg for years now. It was thanks to her mother that I had been able to get into it in the first place. I was one of the "newcomers" Brenda thought so poorly of. The only thing I knew about this camp was that I didn't want to go there.

"You'll be *so* happy you sent Linda to Camp Winnepeg, Mrs. Berman," Brenda said, playing right up to my mother. For some reason grown-ups loved Brenda. I suppose they thought she was pretty, with her big, innocent-looking brown eyes and little, up-turned nose. But when I looked at Brenda, all I saw was her nasty, self-centered personality. All Brenda cared about was her clothes, jewelry, and things like her bird. She loved to make herself look good by making everyone else look bad. Brenda and I lived in

3

the same apartment building, but we didn't get along. We were always fighting over something, and even when I won those fights, it didn't make me happy. It was no fun having an enemy like Brenda.

"I've made some *wonderful* friends here that I've had for years and years!" Brenda continued. "In fact, there are two of them now. Sharon! Melissa! Here I am!" Brenda waved at the two girls. They jumped up and down as if they were actually glad to see her.

I could see why, too. You could tell by the way they dressed, in cute little pastel-colored outfits that were sprinkled with glitter, that Sharon and Melissa were the same type as Brenda Roman. I was dressed in my usual tomboy fashion—shorts cut from old jeans and a baseball T-shirt. I couldn't imagine how anyone could be comfortable in anything else.

Right away I could see I wasn't going to like Sharon and Melissa. Still, I was glad they were there to get Brenda away from me. I wanted nothing more than to be as far from her as I could. But my mother had other ideas.

"Wait, Brenda!" she called as Brenda started toward Sharon and Melissa. "Take Linda with you and introduce her to your friends."

Brenda stopped short, and I could see the conflict in her face. She didn't want to look bad in front of my mother, but I knew she didn't want to introduce me to her precious friends.

I didn't want to be introduced to them, either. Desperately I looked around for a way out. Fortunately I caught sight of Matthew Bainbridge. He was

4

standing by a bus on which there was a sign that said, 10- and 11-Year-Old Groups.

"I'll meet them later, Ma," I said quickly. "Right now I want to say hi to Matt. He's by the bus for my group, so I might as well wait with him."

"Oh, all right." My mother sighed. She never liked the fact that I was a tomboy and preferred to have boys as friends. She went over to talk to Mrs. Roman as Brenda's friends greeted her and Pretty Boy with squeals of delight. I raced over to Matt.

"Matt! I'm so glad you're here! You're the only friendly face around!" Matt was one of my favorite people. He had been in my class in school last year. We became really close over the summer when his dog, Winston, made friends with my cat, Scratchy. When my parents had insisted I give Scratchy away, Matt had been the one to adopt her. It was only because Matt was going to Camp Winnepeg that I had agreed to go.

"Here are some other friendly faces." Matt shook his dark hair out of his brown eyes, the corners of which crinkled with his ready grin. He gestured to the two boys standing next to him. "Sam and Brad, meet Linda. She's really a great guy."

"Guy? She's not a guy!" Sam pointed out.

"She's nothing but a girl!" added Brad.

Of course they were right about this, but that didn't mean I liked them to say it. I looked them over quickly. Sam was thin and on the small side, with sand-colored hair cut in bangs that hung down almost to his blue eyes. Brad had light brown hair and eyes, and he was husky and strong. If it came down to a fight, I figured I could take Sam, but I wasn't sure I could handle Brad.

Still, I wasn't about to show them any fear. "I might be a girl, but I'm as tough as either of you," I said.

"Calm down, Linda. No one's fighting anyone here. We're all going to be friends this summer," Matt said in his easygoing way. "I told you Linda's okay, guys. She can play ball with the best of them. Did you bring your autographed baseball, Linda?"

"I sure did." Proudly I whipped the ball out of my camp bag, in which I had packed some special things for the trip. This ball was my favorite. It was a real baseball, signed by some of the best players on the New York Yankees. My uncle got it when he was on vacation in Florida and went to see the team at spring training. He gave it to me as a gift for my tenth birthday.

"Wow! Let's see that!" Sam and Brad were both very impressed. I let them each hold the ball and examine it carefully. We started talking about which teams we thought would make it to the World Series this year. Then we started talking about sports at Camp Winnepeg, to which the boys had been coming for the last two years.

By the time the camp director, Mr. Hawkins, called us to load the buses, I was starting to really like Sam and Brad. We said goodbye to our parents, and then the four of us found seats together in the back of our bus.

I sat near the window, so I had this great view of Brenda's dramatic leave-taking from Pretty Boy. She

6

actually kissed him goodbye on the tip of his beak before handing him over to her mother. Yuck! I felt sorry for Pretty Boy. I couldn't imagine a fate much worse than being kissed by Brenda!

I was glad to see that Brenda and her friends sat up front, as far from me as possible. I could hear their silly giggling across the entire bus. "Brenda's friends look as disgusting as she is," I commented.

"They are," said Matt. "Everyone knows that Brenda Roman, Sharon Snyder, and Melissa Dillon are the most stuck-up girls in all of Camp Winnepeg. They love to make trouble for other people to make themselves look good."

"And no one can do anything about them," said Sam. "They've been coming here for years and their parents are big shots on the camp board. The counselors play up to those girls. They wind up getting special privileges."

"I don't care what they get, as long as they keep away from me," I said. "I sure hope they don't wind up anywhere near my bunk."

"Near your bunk? They're going to be *in* it," said Brad. "Camp Winnepeg is set up by grade levels. All the boys going into fifth grade are in bunk nine with us. All the girls going to fifth grade are in bunk 109 like you."

I pulled out the paper I had been sent in the mail. It said: Linda Berman, age—ten, bunk assignment—109. "You're right," I groaned. "I'll never make it through the summer if I have to be with girls like that!"

"It's too bad you have to be in a girls' bunk at all,"

7

said Matt. "You'd have a much better time if you could be with us."

"Yeah," agreed Brad. "We boys have better hikes and camp-outs."

"And much better ball games," added Sam. "The girls usually wind up quitting and sitting under some trees in the shade. The boys have much more fun!"

"Boys always have more fun!" I said glumly. "I'd give anything to be able to bunk with you guys. If only there was a way!"

That's when I came up with my plan. I knew it was dangerous and risky and crazy, but I didn't care. It was my one shot at having a good time in camp this summer, and I was going to take it!

Chapter
Two

The Camp Winnepeg buses were scheduled to make a rest stop at the Purple Plum restaurant, halfway to camp. I figured that was when I would set my plan into action.

To make it work, I would need the support of Matt, Sam, and Brad. It was a good thing that we were sitting in the back of the bus. While the rest of the kids sang silly songs, I told my plan to the boys.

"I've got to get switched to your bunk, guys; I've *got* to! And the only way I'm going to get to do it is if everyone thinks I'm a boy."

"How are you going to get everyone to think you're a boy?" asked Brad. "You're registered as Linda Berman. That's a girl's name, and you're assigned to a girls' bunk."

"I'll tell them that's a mistake," I said. "That my real name is *Lindon,* and someone just spelled it

9

wrong, thought I was a girl, and sent me to the wrong bunk."

"What about Brenda Roman?" asked Matt. "She knows you're a girl. She's not going to keep quiet about it."

"I'll take care of Brenda," I said with more confidence than I felt. "She'll be thrilled to have me out of her bunk. Besides, I'll threaten her with a fate worse than death if she squeals."

"Well, even if that would work, you still don't look like a boy," pointed out Sam.

"Not yet. But I brought along my favorite scissors." I pulled them out of my camp bag and grinned. "That's where I need the help of you guys—to give me a short haircut when we park at the rest stop. And, of course, to back up my claim that I really am a boy. If you say you know me from school, Matt, they have to believe me."

"Well, even if your plan works and they put you in our bunk, what are you going to do when it comes time to change for swimming or into pajamas?" asked Sam in his sensible way.

"Oh, don't worry about that. I'll manage to get lost somewhere in the bathroom or behind a tree or something. No one will ever get to see me without my clothes on—I promise. Now, will you guys help me?"

They said they would, so our plan was launched. We were so busy working out the details that before we knew it, we had arrived at the Purple Plum.

"Remember, kids, you have twenty minutes to do as you please. Then I want you back here right on time," Mr. Hawkins warned us in his booming voice that matched his oversize body. He was the kind of person kids obeyed, the perfect camp director.

Everyone piled off the bus and headed for the rest rooms or the snack bar. Everyone except Matt, Brad, Sam, and me. We raced for an area of bushes I spotted at one side of the Purple Plum. There, after I swore them to secrecy in protecting my true identity, I took out my scissors.

"Okay, who's going to give me the haircut?" I asked.

"Not me," said Matt. "I'm not very artistic."

"I'll do it if you want," Sam said shyly.

"I'll do it!" Brad grabbed the scissors from my hand. "I cut my little brother's hair once. Mom was furious, but if you ask me, I thought I did a terrific job. I got everyone to laugh at him, he looked so funny."

"Nobody's asking you, Brad," said Matt. "You're about as clumsy as they come. Let Sam do it."

I looked from Brad's thick, stubby fingers to Sam's thin, graceful ones. "Uh—I think Matt is right, Brad. I can't afford to have everyone laughing at me. I need a haircut that no one will notice."

Brad looked disappointed, but he handed the scissors over to Sam. Sam took his job seriously, snipping carefully from every direction. "Done," he announced finally, stepping back to look me over.

"How do I look?" I asked anxiously.

"Great!" said Matt.

"Sam did a better job than even I could have done," admitted Brad. "No one would know you weren't a boy now."

We had a little time left before we were due back on the bus. Brad went to the snack bar to buy a few candy bars for the trip, while Sam, Matt, and I headed for the bathroom.

Sam and Matt pushed open the door that said Men. Without thinking, I went to the door that said Women.

"Hey, Lin*don,* can't you read?" Matt laughed. "This is the one for boys."

"Oh." I swallowed hard. I hadn't thought about what I was going to do in public rest rooms. "Well, how about checking it out for me first? Let me know if the coast is clear."

Sam poked his head in the door and then back out again. "All clear." He grinned. "It's empty and there are stalls where you can close the door."

I breathed a sigh of relief. I got in and out of that bathroom in record time. I stopped only long enough to glance at myself in the mirror.

Sam really had done a great job on my hair. It wasn't perfectly straight, and it was still slightly on the long side. My big blue eyes did have a feminine look about them, but with some dirt from the bushes smudged across my face and my baseball cap cocked on my head, I almost took myself for a boy!

The next big hurdle was taking care of Brenda. I spotted her standing by some vending machines with Sharon and Melissa. Quickly my mind began racing. I struggled to come up with a plan.

"Matt," I said. "Brenda likes you. How about if you go up to her and tell her you want to talk to her in private? Then you take her to the bushes where we cut my hair. Sam, Brad, and I will be waiting there to lay on the threats."

12

Matt hesitated. "I don't know, Linda. I really don't want to be part of luring Brenda to something bad."

I should have known that Matt was too nice to be a part of anything bad, even when it involved someone who deserved it like Brenda. "Nothing bad is going to happen to her," I promised. "I just have to get her where I can speak to her alone. Come on, Matt. I've got to set things straight with her before we get to camp. This is the only chance I'll get!"

Reluctantly Matt agreed. He walked over to Brenda. Sam and I got Brad and went to hide behind the bushes.

"We only have a few minutes until we have to be back on the bus, Matt," I heard Brenda say as they approached. "So what is it that's so important for you to tell me?"

"This," I said, stepping forward from my hiding place.

Brenda's face grew blank as she stared at me. Then it grew puzzled.

"Linda Berman?" she said. "Is that you? What have you done to yourself? You look like a boy!"

"That's exactly what I intend to look like. From now on Linda Berman no longer exists. As of this moment I am a boy named Lindon Berman. Do you understand?"

"No, I don't understand. What are you trying to pull?"

"I'm trying to have a chance to enjoy myself this summer, which I'm never going to do as long as I'm stuck in some dumb old girls' bunk with you. Look, Brenda, the boys are willing to help me get into their

13

bunk by backing up my story that there was a mistake on my camp forms, and I'm really a boy named Lindon. All I need for this to work is for you to go along with it."

"So you need me for something, do you?" A sneer twisted Brenda's face. "Well, what's in it for me?"

"What's in it for you is that you won't have to deal with me all summer," I told her. "I can make camp life pretty unpleasant for you, you know."

"And we'll help her—I mean him." Brad flexed his muscles so that Brenda would have no doubt what he meant.

"I'm not afraid of you—any of you!" Brenda said. "Mr. Hawkins is friendly with my mom, and he absolutely loves me. All I have to do is go to him and—"

"Do that and Pretty Boy is a memory!" I came out with the threat I had been saving.

"W-what do you mean?" For the first time Brenda looked frightened.

"I mean I'll pull out his feathers one by one!" I said. Of course there was no way I would ever do that to Pretty Boy, but I didn't want Brenda to realize that.

"You—you wouldn't!"

"Oh, so you think I wouldn't? Well, all I have to say to you, Brenda, is don't make me have to prove it. Come on, it's no big deal for you to keep my secret. It'll be better for you. I'll keep out of your way for the whole camp session all summer. How about it?"

Brenda looked at me, then at Matt, Sam, and Brad. She wasn't about to say no in front of the boys. "I'll think about it on the way to camp," she promised.

14

"And now I'm getting back to the bus. I'm not going to start out camp by having Mr. Hawkins mad at me."

She broke into her trotting run that reminded me of a penguin's. The boys and I laughed to see her, then Sam looked at his watch.

"Hey, we really should be getting back to the bus," he said.

We made it to the bus just as Mr. Hawkins was blowing his whistle for the final call to load up. He glared at us angrily. "You boys are the last ones back."

I didn't even mind. He had included me as one of the boys, and that was what mattered. My plan was going to work!

Chapter
Three

Welcome to Camp Winnepeg. My heart leaped as the bus drove under the sign and up the long, tree-lined driveway that led to the heart of camp. We were here, and now was the time I would find out if my plan was going to work. Our bus stopped near the other buses, in front of the main dining room. There the campers were to meet with their counselors and go to their assigned bunks.

It was another scene of mass chaos. Bewildered kids piled off the buses, trying to find their belongings and their counselors. The counselors stood in a row, holding up signs for their groups. I followed the boys to the sign that said bunk 9, ten-year-old boys. I tried to ignore the fact that bunk 109, ten-year-old girls, was forming right next to me.

"Hi, guys, I'm Greg, your counselor for the summer," the tall, thin, college-age boy holding the sign announced. "And this is Jeff, my assistant." He pointed to the dark, shorter boy standing next to him. "Listen up and check in with me while Jeff reads out our group list to make sure you're all in the right place."

It was hard to hear over the noise the other kids were making, but I was able to make out Matt's name, and Brad's and Sam's, and that of the other seven boys in the group. Of course my name wasn't called.

"Did I get everybody?" Greg asked when he had finished.

I took a deep breath and crossed my fingers for good luck. "I don't think you called me," I said.

"I didn't? Well, what's your name?"

"Lindon. Lindon Berman."

"That's funny. There's no Lindon Berman on my list. Maybe you're assigned to someone else's bunk. Hey, anyone got a Lindon Berman on their camper list?"

"Lindon Berman? That's strange. There's a Linda Berman on my list who hasn't shown up yet," said the counselor of bunk 109 as she walked up to our group. She had long straight blond hair and was very pretty. "My name is Aileen. Do you have a twin sister or something, Lindon?"

All attention was now focused on me. My heart was pounding. I knew that the way I acted in the next few moments would either make or break my stay at Camp Winnepeg. I had to convince everyone I was really a boy.

"Oh, no, not again!" I threw my hands up to my

17

head and shook it. "This is always happening to me. Why did my parents have to give me a name like Lindon? People are always hearing it as Linda and thinking I'm a girl. I've had more problems straightening out my records in school. I hope this isn't going to be any kind of trouble. Getting me off the bunk 109 list and onto the bunk nine list, I mean."

"It shouldn't be—there's room for twelve in my bunk," said Greg. "I'll go straighten it out with Mr. Hawkins." He walked over to where Mr. Hawkins was standing, leafing through piles of papers and trying to answer questions from kids and counselors.

"Hawkins is too busy to deal with this now," Greg reported when he returned. "He said for you to come along to bunk 9, and he'll correct the paperwork when he has more time."

This was exactly what I wanted to hear. I exchanged joyful looks with Matt, Brad, and Sam and followed along with the rest of the boys up the hill to our bunk. I turned around once to find Brenda Roman standing with her group and staring after me. I was so glad to be rid of Brenda and her dumb old girls' bunk, I didn't care if I risked getting her angry. I screwed up my face and stuck my tongue out at her. It felt perfectly wonderful to do it!

The bunkhouses were set deep in the trees and were made of logs. The walls and floors were wooden, and wood cabinets lined the walls. I could squint my eyes and pretend I was in a log cabin somewhere in the wilderness. I loved it right away.

"Find a cabinet and unpack your things, boys," Greg announced. "Then go choose a bunk bed and relax until we start the first activity. And let's not have any fighting over who wants uppers and lowers."

I raced to unpack as quickly as possible so I would be sure to get an upper bunk. Fortunately, Sam and Matt both liked lowers, so Brad and I took the uppers above them. Also fortunately, the bunk Matt and I chose was in the corner, so there was no one on one side of us. With Brad and Sam in the next bunk, I was well set off from the rest of the group.

"You guys want to read my comic books?" offered Sam.

He had brought up a whole stack of comics. We all picked out something interesting and lay back in our bunks to read. It was amazing to me how well the four of us got along. I had always liked having boys as friends. Getting into the boys' bunk was one of the best moves I had ever made. I was really feeling great about things—safe and warm and comfortable.

"Okay, boys, don't get too lazy—time for our first swim." Greg announced. "Change into your swimsuits and come out on the porch with your towels."

Instantly my good feelings disappeared. "Swim-suits—uh-oh, I didn't think about that," I whispered to the boys. "I only have a girl's bathing suit."

"I have an extra suit I could let you borrow," said Sam.

I took it from him, grateful that he was close to my

size. "Thanks. I—uh—think I'd better head for the bathroom to change."

I got into a stall and squirmed into the suit, which fit me fine. I threw a T-shirt on over it. Even though I had nothing to hide, there was no way I was going outside with nothing on top.

I felt very self-conscious as we headed down to the lake, but no one seemed to notice me. I began to relax.

"Everyone stay in the shallow roped-off section of the lake for today," Greg called out. "Tomorrow we'll have swim tests to see who's good enough to swim in the deep water."

There were some groans of protest at this but not from me. Swimming wasn't my greatest skill, and I was just as glad to stay inside the ropes.

I was about to jump in when I heard loud, shrill giggling and shouting. "Ohh! The water is so cold! It tickles!" I turned around and saw the girls of bunk 109 invading the lake.

"Hey! What are these girls doing here? It's supposed to be our swim time!" I protested to Greg.

"Our swim time and their swim time, too," he replied. "Since you're all the same age, our bunk does a lot of activities together with bunk 109. You might as well get used to it."

"Oh, great," I groaned as I watched Brenda, Sharon, and Melissa approach the water. I was tempted to rush up behind Brenda and push her in, but I controlled myself. I didn't want to do anything that might cause her to squeal on me.

I kept out of Brenda's way, but she didn't keep out of mine. "Hey, Lin!" she called when she spotted me. "Why don't you take off your T-shirt when you go into the water?"

I glared at her. "You know perfectly well why, Brenda. It's because I get sunburned so easily!"

"Sunburn! That's a laugh! Your skin is as tough as a rhinocerous hide!"

"Rhinoceros hide!" I was furious. "You'd better watch what you say to me Brenda Roman, or else—"

"Or else what, Linda—I mean Lindon Berman?"

Brenda's slip of the tongue brought me back to reality. I needed her to keep my secret. I couldn't afford to give her what she deserved when it was so easy for her to get back at me by telling everyone my true identity. So, painful as it was, I turned my back to her and plunged into the water. I kept as far away from her and her friends as was possible in that small, roped-off area.

After swim we had some free time before dinner. Sam and Brad challenged Matt and me to a friendly game of rummy. We were sprawled out on the lower bunks, and I was thinking how lucky I was to have gotten in with these great guys, when Greg tapped me on the shoulder.

"Mr. Hawkins is ready to speak to you now. He's waiting for you at the main office."

My stomach clutched when he said this. If it was only a matter of fixing up the paperwork, why would Mr. Hawkins have to see me in his office? Could something have gone wrong?

21

I told myself not to be silly, that this interview with Mr. Hawkins was going to be routine. Still, my heart pounded as I approached his office.

As soon as I pushed open the door and walked inside, I knew my worst fears were realized. For there, sitting on a chair in front of Mr. Hawkins's big desk, was Brenda Roman with a very smug look on her face!

Chapter
Four

Mr. Hawkins looked from me over to Brenda, then back to me again. "Sit down, Linda," he boomed in a voice that set my nerves tingling.

I was about to open my mouth for one last protest, but he stopped me short. "No, don't say a word. I just had a little conversation with Brenda to try to get to the bottom of this, and I think we have. This is the same Linda Berman that lives in your apartment building, isn't it, Brenda?"

Brenda stared me right in the eyes and nodded her head. "Yes, it is, Mr. Hawkins. She cut her hair to look like a boy, that's all."

"Thank you, Brenda. That's enough. You may go back to your bunk now."

"But—" Brenda's attempted protest was cut short by a look from Mr. Hawkins. Reluctantly she got up from her chair and left the room. I was sure she was burning up inside that Mr. Hawkins wouldn't let her stay to watch what he was going to do.

"Sit down, Linda," he repeated. I sat in the chair that Brenda had vacated. Next to huge Mr. Hawkins and his oversize desk, I felt very small, helpless, and afraid of what was to come. I looked down and studied my feet, which didn't even reach the floor.

"Well, Linda, in my eighteen years of working in camps, I don't think I've ever had to deal with a situation like this," Mr. Hawkins said. "Whatever made you pull something like pretending you were a boy?"

What made me? I was sure Mr. Hawkins would never understand. Still, once I began trying to explain it to him, I found I couldn't stop until I told him the whole story.

I told him how I hadn't wanted to go to camp in the first place, especially because it meant being with Brenda and other stuck-up girls like her. I told him how well I got along with Matthew and his friends and how I liked to play boys' games and sports. I told him how I was so sure I would be much happier in bunk 9 than in bunk 109 that I was willing to take the chance of cutting my hair and trying to pass for a boy.

"Matt, Brad, and Sam are my friends," I finished. "Wouldn't you want to be together with your friends if you were away at camp?" I sat there staring miserably at my feet again. I waited for Mr. Hawkins's angry words.

He was silent for what seemed a very long time. When he finally did start to speak, his voice was so calm and quiet that it startled me into looking up at him.

"Why, yes, I suppose I would want to be with my friends," he admitted, running his hand through his dark curly hair. "And you will be with them more than you think. You'll have quite a few activities together with bunk 9."

"But what about the times we won't be together?" I asked. "I can't stand to be with those girls!"

"How do you know that?" he demanded. "Just because you don't like Brenda, it doesn't mean you won't like her friends or the other girls in the bunk. You haven't even met them yet."

"But I never like girls as much as I like boys."

"Probably because you don't give them a chance. You're a girl, Linda, and cutting your hair short isn't going to change that. Isn't it better for you to accept it and learn to get along with the other girls?"

"Why? If you let me stay in bunk 9 with the boys, there will be no problem."

"Maybe not with you, but you can be sure some of the other boys and their parents would object if they found out. No, Linda, I'm afraid you're going to have to accept your assignment to bunk 109 and make the best of it!"

Make the best of it. That was easier said than done. Mr. Hawkins called for Carol, the assistant counselor of bunk 109, to come help me get my things and make the transfer.

As soon as we left Mr. Hawkins's office, Carol began

to laugh so hard I thought her ribs would break. I looked at her strangely. I didn't even know what she was laughing about.

"Boy, I wish I could have seen Hawkins's face when he found out you had fooled him by pretending that you were a boy," she said when she finally caught her breath. "That was a wild thing for you to do. Do you know I thought about doing something like that once or twice when I was your age?"

"You did?" I looked at her again. Carol had a sweet face, shoulder-length wavy brown hair, and didn't seem like a tomboy type.

"Sure. I was a bit of a tomboy, myself, then. I liked playing ball and preferred boys' games to girls'. I always thought that boys had more fun."

"So what happened? You don't look like a tomboy now."

"I started growing up. I found some girls I really liked as friends, girls I could talk to about anything. I began to be interested in boys in a different way—as boyfriends, not just as friends. I discovered the good points about being a girl."

"What are those? I can't find any."

Carol laughed again. "I'm afraid you're going to have to find that out for yourself. Keep an open mind, Linda. This summer could turn out better than you expect."

"I doubt it," I grumbled. "I bet the girls in bunk 109 have been programmed by Brenda to hate me already."

When I got to the bunkhouse, the girls were outside

with Aileen, playing board games on the porch. They stared at me as if I were a freak.

"What's the matter, haven't you ever seen a girl with short hair before?" I demanded angrily.

No one answered, but I heard lots of giggling as I turned my back to them and walked inside. "You see, I'll never get along with anyone in this bunk!" I complained to Carol, who had followed me inside the cabin. It looked pretty much the same as the boys' bunk did.

"They don't hate you. They just don't know what to make of a girl who looks like a boy. Give them a chance to get to know you, and they'll forget about your hair, which, fortunately, will start to grow again. And you forget about it, too. All you have to do is make up your mind to have a good time at camp, and you will."

"I doubt it. Anyhow, where do I put my things?"

"Cabinet ten is empty. So is bed ten, over there in the corner. I hope you don't mind an upper."

"Mind? No, I love an upper. It's the only break I've had since I came to this camp. But who's sleeping under me?"

"I am," a voice squeaked.

I looked and saw a girl staring at me with shy, blue-green eyes. She was small and thin and had pale skin and a mop of curly red hair. She was cute-looking, but you could see she was the type that other kids would love to pick on.

"Who are you?" I asked.

It took so long for the girl to reply that Carol wound

27

up doing it for her. "That's Farah. Farah Barton. She's new here, the only one in this bunk that hasn't been to camp Winnepeg before, besides you, Linda. She doesn't know anyone, either. Maybe you two can be friends."

Farah smiled at me shyly, but she still didn't say a word. She looked so weak and puny that I couldn't imagine her hitting a baseball or playing a game out in the sun without wilting.

Great, I couldn't help thinking. I had started out this day as one of the boys. I had ended it with my only chance for a friend being this little redheaded girl. My chances of having a good time in camp this summer looked worse than ever!

Chapter
Five

I woke up the next morning to the unfamiliar sound of birds chirping. I opened my eyes and saw the shadows of leaves moving across the rough wood of the ceiling. For a moment I didn't know where I was.

Then it all came back to me. Camp. I was stuck here in bunk 109 with Brenda Roman and some dumb old girls.

"Everyone up! Everyone up!" Aileen's far-too-cheerful voice sang out. "We've got a bunk meeting before breakfast. You've got fifteen minutes to go to the bathroom, get dressed, and meet me out on the porch!"

"Fifteen minutes!" I complained to Farah as I swung down off my top bunk. "You'd think we were in the army or something!"

By the time I got to the bathroom, there was a line of six girls waiting to get into the three stalls. Everyone else was fighting to get a spot at the sinks to wash up and brush their teeth.

"The early bird gets the worm—or in this case first shot at the bathroom," Brenda said nastily as she walked by my spot at the end of the line. She looked perfectly gorgeous, and it didn't take me long to find out why. In her hand she carried a blow-dryer. It was just like Brenda to bother taking a blow-dryer to camp. I wondered how early she had gotten up in order to have enough time to fuss with herself.

I was splashing some cold water on my sleepy face when Brenda stuck her head back in the door. "What's taking you so long, Linda? Aileen's called a bunk meeting, remember? Everyone's waiting for you. If you don't hurry up, we'll be late for breakfast, and it'll be all your fault!"

"All my fault! If everyone else hadn't taken so darn long in the bathroom, I would have been done and—!"

But Brenda didn't wait around to listen. She stuck her tongue out at me and disappeared from the doorway.

I quickly ran my toothbrush over my teeth and my comb through what was left of my light brown hair. I hurried out into the bunk area to find everyone sitting around the big table in the center of the room.

"Hurry up and get dressed, Linda; we're waiting for you," Aileen said with a sigh.

"I always thought boys took less time to get ready than girls did," commented Brenda.

I felt very self-conscious as I struggled into my

30

shorts. I knew everyone was watching me, and I didn't like it.

"Next time get up earlier if it takes you so long to get ready," said Aileen as I joined the others around the table.

"It wouldn't have taken me so long if—" I began to protest, but no one seemed interested in what I had to say. I could see by the looks on the girls' faces that none of them liked me. Boy, did I hate this camp! It was even worse than I thought it would be!

"All right girls, now we can *finally* begin," said Aileen. "I want to tell the newcomers and remind those of you who have been here before about how things are done here at Camp Winnepeg. First of all, we have a basic schedule of activities for each day that will include arts and crafts, swimming, boating, and sports." She passed around a paper that had the day divided into blocks of time with the activities written in. "I'll put this up on the bulletin board where you can refer to it when necessary. For now, let's start getting our chores."

"Chores! Don't tell me we still have to do stuff like cleaning and serving!" Brenda broke in. "My mother told me she was going to speak to Mr. Hawkins and fix it so we campers didn't have to do that kind of work."

"That kind of work won't do you any harm," Aileen replied. "It's good for everyone to have a sense of responsibility and do some work for the common good. So, what I want you to do is to divide yourself up into three groups. I'll assign each group a task. There's bathroom cleanup, bunk cleanup, and serving

31

and cleaning up after meals. We'll rotate these chores weekly so everyone gets a chance to do everything."

"We want to be together," Brenda said, pointing to her shadows, Sharon and Melissa.

"We'll be a group." Three of the other girls, Debbie, Karen, and Cindy, joined up.

That left me, Farah, and two other girls, Heather and Rachel, who I had noticed didn't seem to fit in with the others. "I guess that means the four of us are stuck together," Rachel said.

"Hey, that's not fair!" Brenda cried. "They get to divide their work up four ways, and we only get to do it three ways."

"Well, Brenda, you could have asked a fourth person to join your group," said Aileen. "The three of you don't have to always be by yourselves."

I loved hearing Aileen put Brenda down. But my good feelings didn't last. They ended when I found out the first chore our group was given. Cleaning the bathroom—yuck, yuck, yuck!

It was a tradition at Camp Winnepeg for everyone to gather on the hill in front of the dining room before each meal. There, we would listen to announcements and sing camp songs while Greg played the guitar.

"I want everyone to try to sing along with me as best you can," said Greg. "After a few days you'll get to know the songs and the words to them."

Greg began with a folksong called "If I Had a Hammer." As everyone started singing, I spotted Matt, Brad, and Sam. I walked over to them.

32

"How's it going over at bunk 109?" Matt asked.

"Well, let's put it this way. If I had a hammer, I would hammer on Brenda Roman's beautifully blow-dried and stuck-up head," I told him. "Besides that, my counselors are okay, and there are a few girls in the bunk who don't seem that bad. But too many of them are too much like Brenda. I can't imagine how we're going to get a game of baseball going, or any other sport for that matter!"

"Why don't you ask if you could join our bunk for sports?" said Sam.

"Yeah, we can always use a good player on our team," said Brad.

"Do you mean it, guys?" I felt unexpected tears burning my eyes. I pretended to have some dirt in them so the boys wouldn't notice. It made me feel great to be accepted by Matt, Brad, and Sam.

"Sure we mean it," said Matt. "It shouldn't be a problem because your bunk is scheduled for sports the same time ours is. But we've got to go about it right this time. Why don't you ask your counselor if you can be part of our bunk, just for sports?"

"I'll do that!" I said excitedly. "It might be the very thing that would work for me!"

I went to Carol with my idea. She was sympathetic, but she wasn't very encouraging.

"Play sports with bunk 9? It sounds okay, but I'm not sure Hawkins will go along with it. After all, you haven't even given sports with your own group a chance, Linda. Look, we've got softball scheduled for today. Why don't you give it a shot and see how it goes? If you're not happy, I'll ask Aileen to talk to Hawkins about your idea."

I did as Carol suggested and went along for the first softball game. It was our bunk against the girls of bunk 110, who were a year older than we were. That wasn't fair to begin with. Still, we would have had a chance if only the girls on my team made half an effort. But Brenda and her friends were more interested in what was going on in the next field than in our own. That's where the boys from bunk 9 were playing against the eleven-year-old boys from bunk 10.

I wouldn't have minded so much if it was the boys' ball game the girls were interested in. I could understand that. The boys were really trying and made some great plays. But once I heard some of the girls' conversation, I realized that the game was the last thing on their minds.

"Ooh, look at Sam make that catch! I think he's so-oo cute!" said Sharon as she waited for her chance to bat.

"How about that Brad? Did you see how hard he swung that bat?" Melissa broke in.

"If you ask me, the cutest one is that new boy, Jed Lalotta," squealed Brenda. "I absolutely *adore* boys who are tall and blond!"

Once they started, it wasn't long before the rest of the girls were busy discussing the boys on the next field. No one seemed the least bit interested in playing ball.

"Hey! Who's up next?" I demanded finally. "This is supposed to be a ball game!"

"Oh, cut it out, Linda," complained Brenda. "You

34

don't understand things like the importance of good-looking boys."

"Not when we're supposed to be playing ball," I protested, but no one paid attention to what I said. It was only when Rachel, who had managed to get on third base, began to call out that she was in danger of getting sunstroke out there on the field that Aileen bothered to tell Heather to get to the batter's cage.

It was our one chance to score the whole game, but Heather didn't quite make it. She hit a high pop-up ball, and our team was out.

No one seemed to care that we lost the game, but I did. I couldn't stand the thought of this kind of thing going on all through camp. I had to get to play ball with the boys—I *had* to. This was too important for me to trust to Aileen.

I would have to speak to Mr. Hawkins myself.

Chapter
Six

As soon as the game was over, I snuck away from my group and raced up to Mr. Hawkins's office. He looked at me as if I were the last kid in camp he wanted to see. "Now what?" he asked with a sigh.

"This is just a small request," I assured him quickly. "I'd like to be part of bunk 9 for sports period only. Playing ball with a bunch of girls who are only interested in watching the boys is a total waste!"

"A total waste, is it?" Mr. Hawkins appeared to be stifling a laugh. "Well, I'll think about your request, Linda, and I'll let you know."

I felt good about my chances of winning on this issue as I joined my group for the next activity, which was arts and crafts. Aileen came rushing up to me as if I had done something wrong.

"Where were you, Linda?" she demanded. "I couldn't find you anywhere after the game!"

"Oh, I had something important to talk to Mr. Hawkins about," I told her.

"Linda! I don't care if you had something important to discuss with the Queen of England! You can't go running off by yourself without letting me know first. This is camp, and I'm your counselor—I'm responsible for you. Do you understand?"

Aileen was so angry her face flushed red. I couldn't understand why. "I was only gone about twenty minutes," I pointed out. "What did you think could happen to me in that amount of time?"

"Anything could happen to you in that amount of time!" Aileen said. "Look, Linda, just make sure that nothing like this ever happens again!"

"Okay, okay," I promised. I went into the arts building to see what my group was doing. Art, at least, was something I had always been good at. I loved to paint and draw and make different things. And I didn't see where I could get into trouble with art!

After art was lunch, then we had a quiet period for reading, playing games, or writing letters. Aileen insisted that we write a postcard home to our parents.

I stared at my postcard miserably. What could I possibly write home that would sound cheerful and not be a complete lie? Certainly not that I was getting along with everyone, had lots of friends, and was a favorite among my counselors. Only one day had gone by, and the fact was that I had already become the black sheep of Camp Winnepeg. I wrote that the countryside was beautiful and the food was basically okay.

37

I was struggling to think of something else to say when Carol announced it was time to get ready for swim. There it was, the perfect ending for my card. "Time to get ready for swim," I wrote in letters big enough to fill up the rest of the space.

I got into my bathing suit as fast as I could, but I didn't have to worry about holding up the group this time. Brenda, Sharon, and Melissa were taking so long deciding which of their many suits to put on that everyone else was ready before they had even gotten undressed.

"Come on, girls, the rest of us are ready to go," Carol urged them.

"We're trying to decide which suits do the most for our figures," said Brenda.

"The boys will be there, and we want to look our best!" added Sharon.

Carol let out a deep sigh. "I'm sure you'll look great no matter which suits you put on. Hurry up now, okay?"

After that fuss you would think the girls would have wound up looking spectacular. Instead, they appeared in suits that looked like the rest of the clothes they always wore—pastel colors and glitter. They didn't look so great to me. I couldn't even imagine how they could swim in suits like that.

The one who did look spectacular was Aileen. She wore a white bikini, which set off her slim but curvy figure. With her tan skin, blue eyes, and long blond hair, she looked like a model in a magazine.

I couldn't help staring. And wondering. Would I get to look like that some day? For the first time the

38

thought entered my mind that maybe it might not be so bad to be a girl, at least not a girl who looked like Aileen.

I went to the bathroom to check the mirror. I frowned. I certainly didn't look anything like Aileen. I had pretty big blue eyes and my figure was okay—I wasn't too fat or too thin. But I was short and there was no sign of even the beginning of curves. My old black and white checkered bathing suit did nothing for me whatsoever.

Now I was sorry that I hadn't gotten a new suit before the start of camp. My mother had offered to buy me one, but I hated to go shopping so much that I told her I would make do with my old ones. Now, with the sun shining so brightly, I could see that the material was starting to look faded and worn. This was not something that ordinarily would have bothered me, but for some reason it did. I thought of changing to my other suit, but Aileen poked her head into the bathroom.

"Aren't you ready yet, Linda? It seems we're always waiting for you."

"I was ready a long time ago," I started to explain. But Aileen was heading out to the porch and not listening. Was I going to get blamed for everything that happened in bunk 109?

It was no surprise that the boys were already there when we finally got down to the lake. The day was hot, and I was so eager to get into the water that I raced ahead of my group. I caught sight of Matt, Brad, and Sam already in the water, and I jumped in to join them. "Hi, guys!" I said happily. "Boy, am I glad we have swim together with you!"

Before anyone could reply, I felt a strong hand grab on to my arm. I whirled around and saw it was Scott, the swimming counselor, glaring at me.

"And what do you think you're doing? Can't you see I'm giving these guys their swimming test? Get out of the water right now!"

Confused, I did as he asked. I saw the girls from my bunk sitting in a row on the dock. They were laughing, and I knew it was at me.

"Linda! What's the matter with you?" asked Aileen. "Didn't you hear me say that no one was to go into the water today until you were tested to see how well you could swim?"

"No-oo, I didn't," I said meekly.

"Gees." She shook her long blond hair. "You'd better start listening before you wind up in real trouble! Now, go sit with the other girls and wait your turn!"

I sat down on the grass away from everyone else. There was no one in this group who liked me, no one I wanted to talk to, anyhow.

I watched Scott give the swim tests. To make Advanced Swim and go in the deep water, you had to be able to do eight laps in the area between the two docks that jutted out into the lake. In addition, you had to show that you could keep yourself afloat, doing strokes like the dog paddle, for five minutes. To make the Intermediate Swim, which meant you could swim in water up to your head, you had to do two laps and stay afloat for one minute. If you couldn't do that, you were stuck in Beginner Swim, in water no more than three feet deep.

Swimming was not my best sport. I never had the chance to practice enough to get good at it. I knew there was no way I would make Advanced, but I was pretty sure I could manage the two laps for Intermediate.

The test was a lot more difficult than I thought it would be. It had been so long since I had gone swimming, I found myself getting tired fast. That last half-lap seemed to stretch a mile. I was panting and struggling until I finally was able to grab on to the dock.

"Intermediate," Scott called as I pulled myself out of the water. It felt great to hear it. My first success since my arrival at camp!

"Sharon, Melissa, and I made Advanced," Brenda gloated. I ignored her, but I couldn't any more when I saw her go over to tease Farah.

Farah was having a hard time taking her swim test. She was standing in water that came up only to her waist. Her pale skin had turned blue, and her teeth were chattering. She hugged her arms to her body and seemed absolutely petrified.

"Just put your face in," Scott urged. "You can hold on to the dock; you don't have to let go. If you put your face in, you'll see that the water won't hurt you."

"No! I can't! I'm afraid!" Farah said.

"But it's only water," said Scott. "Here, let me show you." He cupped some water in his hand and sprinkled it over Farah's head.

That was the wrong thing to do with Farah. She let

41

out a scream, turned around, and went splashing out of the lake.

"All right, Farah, all right," Scott called. "It's Beginner for you."

"Beginner Swim—unbelievable!" Brenda taunted Farah. "You're a disgrace to our bunk! Why don't you get yourself transferred to a baby group?"

Farah's face went white. Her lip trembled, and it looked as if she would start to cry right there. I knew how embarrassed she must feel. Without thinking, I stepped between her and Brenda.

"Why don't you go practice your fancy swimming strokes, Brenda?" I suggested. "With a little luck, maybe you'll lose yourself somewhere in the deep water."

"You're just jealous, Linda," she said haughtily. She strutted across the dock and dived into the water, leaving Farah and me alone.

"Th-thanks, Linda," Farah said gratefully.

"No problem. Any time you want to get rid of Brenda, I'll be glad to help. She thinks she's so hot because she knows how to swim well. If it weren't for the fact her parents are rich and sent her for private swimming lessons, I bet she wouldn't be any better than we are."

"Y-you don't swim so badly. I saw you make Intermediate. I'll never be able to do that."

"Sure you will," I told her. "I was afraid of the water for a long time myself until two years ago. I had a bad experience with water when I was little."

"You did? What happened?"

"Well, it was in a swimming pool my parents had

42

taken me to. I was having a great time, splashing about in water about up to my chest. Then someone bumped into me and I went under. It was the weirdest sensation. Instead of being above the water looking down, suddenly I was below it looking up.

"It was actually pretty neat at first. The light looked pretty filtering through the water, and people's bodies came drifting by. But then I found I couldn't get up again, and I needed air. I began to panic."

"Oh, no!" gasped Farah. "What did you do?"

"I pushed down on the floor really hard and moved my arms in swimming motions. Somehow, I managed to get up to the surface and get my feet back on the floor. I got out of the pool as fast as I could and didn't want to go back in again."

"That's what happened to me," Farah said so softly that I could hardly hear her.

"What? What happened to you?"

"I slipped into the water once and couldn't get back up again. But I really did almost drown. I had to have someone pull me out and give me artificial respiration, and I got sick and was throwing up. It was so awful I never wanted to go in water above my waist ever again!"

"I could see why you feel that way," I said. "But you can get over that. When I told my father about what had happened to me, he made me get right back into the water so I would lose my fear of it. That summer he taught me how to swim, enough so I would no longer be afraid. I'm still very careful about anything that has to do with water. But I've gotten to the point where swimming is fun for me again."

43

"I don't think I could ever get to that point," Farah said. "To tell you the truth, I didn't even want to come to camp this summer because I was afraid they would make me go underwater. But my parents told me my fears were nonsense and I had to go."

"Your fears aren't nonsense. It's very scary to almost drown. I know because it almost happened to me. I'll tell you what. Scott will let us in for free swim soon. If you want, I'll come into the shallow water with you and show you how my father taught me to swim. It was very slow and not scary at all."

"You—you won't do anything like make me put my face in the water, will you?"

"Of course not. I'll teach you exactly the way I would want to be taught if it were me."

"Promise?"

"Promise."

Farah smiled at me. It was a great feeling to be appreciated for a change. For the first time since being put in bunk 109, I almost felt good about being in Camp Winnepeg.

Chapter
Seven

The next day during chore time, when I was in the midst of cleaning up the mess Brenda Roman had left by splashing water all over the bathroom sink, Carol came in to tell me that Mr. Hawkins wanted to see me.

This time I went to his office feeling confident. I was sure this had to do with my request to be allowed to play ball with the boys of bunk 9. I was sure there would be no problem with something so simple.

I was wrong. Mr. Hawkins looked up from his desk. "I'm afraid I can't allow you to join the boys' teams."

"But—but why not?"

"Because the boys' bunk wouldn't all agree to it. One of them was against it."

"But who? And why?"

"I'm not going to tell you who, but I will tell you why. He didn't think it was right to have one girl on a boys' team."

45

"What difference could it possibly make to him?"

"Well, he's one of those boys who likes everything masculine and tough. I guess having a girl on his team didn't fit in with his image."

"But that's silly. I can play ball as well as any boy. There's no reason to keep me off the team. That's sex discrimination!"

"You have a point there, Linda, and don't think I haven't been giving thought to your situation. The policy of separating boys and girls for sports at Camp Winnepeg is an old one. It dates back years and years, from when the camp was first started. We're living in modern times now, a time of equal opportunity for all. I've decided that the era of separation should belong to the past. As a result, from now on I'm going to be merging sports activities for boys and girls of the same age."

"You are?" I was absolutely amazed. "But a moment ago you said you weren't going to let me play on the boys' team because someone objected."

"Objected to having only you play, which was one matter. No one can object to having the boys' and girls' teams merge, because that's now camp policy."

I walked out of Mr. Hawkins's office in a daze. Boys' and girls' teams merging together. Without even trying, I had accomplished something. For a change. I was really proud of myself!

The first reaction to the new camp policy was not what I hoped it would be. "We don't want to have sports with the boys," complained Brenda.

"They're way too rough," said Sharon.

"We'd rather watch them play than play with them," said Melissa.

"Girls, girls, that's enough now," warned Carol. "Give the idea of co-ed sports a try. You might find you like it."

The girls' complaints were one thing. The boys' complaints were far worse. Groans and protests rang out as soon as we arrived at the field for the day's softball game.

"Girls! We don't want to have to play with girls on our team! Whose idea was this?"

I said nothing. It really wasn't my idea, but Mr. Hawkins's, anyhow.

"It must have been Linda Berman's idea!" Jed Lalotta piped up. He was the boy Brenda thought was the cutest thing in camp. The problem was that Jed also thought he was the cutest thing in camp. He was as conceited as they come.

"For your information, Jed, it was not my idea," I told him.

"It had to have been. Mr. Hawkins asked us yesterday to vote on letting you be on our team. The rest of the guys would have gone along with that dumb idea, too, if I hadn't said no way."

"Oh, so you're the one who voted against me."

"Of course I voted against you." Jed's face was so red with anger now that he didn't even look cute anymore. "Girls are girls and boys are boys. The ballfield is not the place where they should mix."

"Oh, listen to him," said Rachel. "A real big shot."

47

"We'll show you that we can play as good a game of softball as you can," said Heather.

I was happy to have their support, but before anyone could say anything else, Aileen came over. "Okay, kids. Let's stop this bickering and get the ball game rolling. Greg and I made up teams we thought were a fair mixture of boys and girls together. Everyone will be assigned to either the red team or the blue team for all co-ed sports. Now listen while I call out your name for your team assignment."

Good luck was shining on me. I got on the blue team with the boys I liked: Matt, Brad, and Sam. Not only that, the only girls I could stand were on my team as well: Farah, Heather, and Rachel. Having the disgusting job of cleaning the bathroom together had drawn the four of us closer together.

"Isn't that cute?" Brenda said with a sneer. "The entire 'Bathroom Brigade' is on the same team."

"Yes, and we'll make you 'Glitter Girls' wish you were on our team before camp is over," I said. Brenda and her friends had all gotten on the red team, along with Jed. Nothing would give me greater pleasure than to have our team put their team to shame.

Carol and Greg were our team's coaches. They assigned us fielding positions and made up the batting order. I got on base the first two times at bat, and I hit in a run on my third. I also made two great plays in my position as third baseman—I mean basewoman.

Every time I did something right, I noticed Jed's face get redder and redder. You could see he was furious that I was playing so well. But the best came at the end of the game. Our team was ahead by one run. There was one out, Jed was on second, and this kid, Kevin, who was a powerful hitter, was up at bat. If both Jed and Kevin scored, we would lose the game.

Kevin hit a line drive to first and was out. Brad, the first baseman, threw the ball to me. I made this great catch and managed to tag Jed as he slid into third base.

"Out!" called Jeff, the counselor who was umpiring. "That's the game."

"Out? What do you mean, 'out'?" Jed protested. "Are you blind or something? I was safe by a mile."

"Oh, no, you weren't," I said. "I tagged you right before your foot touched base."

"Impossible! No girl is faster than I am!"

"Well, this one is this time! You were out by a mile!"

"Enough of that, kids," said Jeff. "It was a really close play, but I'm the umpire, and I say you were out, Jed. That's all there is to it. That's three outs for your team, and the game is over. Blue team is the winner." He turned and walked away, leaving Jed and me glaring at each other.

"You think you're so great, Linda, but I know better. Jeff gave you the benefit of the doubt because you're a girl. If you and I had a contest head to head, I'd win hands down."

"Oh, yeah? Is that a challenge?"

"Yes, it is. I can beat you at any one-on-one activity there is—wrestling, weight lifting, racing . . ."

"So what if you could?" I shrugged. "Those are all activities that need size and strength, and you're bigger and stronger than I am. That's not what counts. It's skill that makes the difference."

"Skill? Okay, so we'll find something that requires skill. And to show you how big I am, I'll let you pick the activity. What'll it be?"

My mind raced, trying to come up with something where Jed wouldn't have the advantage. Kids were starting to gather around us now, so there would be witnesses to whatever I said. I looked around and focused on some large trees behind the ballfield—trees with large, sturdy limbs that were great for climbing. Climbing trees was something I always loved to do. I wished I could be up there now, reaching for the clear blue sky, away from nonsense like trying to prove something to jerks like Jed.

"Tree climbing," I said.

"What?"

"We'll have a tree-climbing contest. See who can climb the highest and fastest."

"I don't know about that," Jed said. "It's against camp rules to climb trees. Insurance and all that. Hawkins would be furious if he caught us."

"So we don't let him catch us. You told me I could pick the activity. Are you chickening out?"

Jed looked around at our audience and played directly to them. "Of course not," he said, making his voice as deep as he could. "I just need some time to work out the details. We'll have our contest during free time tomorrow night."

50

"Fine." I turned to leave, but his voice stopped me.

"And Linda, one more thing."

"What's that?"

"I intend to totally humiliate you." His eyes flashed anger. I knew he meant business.

Chapter Eight

The free-time period after dinner was the least supervised time at Camp Winnepeg. Most of the time kids hung out on the porches of the bunkhouses, playing games and writing letters. As long as we were back for the start of evening activity, we were also allowed to walk around the grounds on our own. It was the one time when the counselors weren't constantly aware of where we were. It was the only time we could get away with having our contest.

Jed and I decided to meet at the big trees at the edge of the ballfield at seven o'clock. He was supposed to bring his supporters, and I was to bring mine.

I asked Matt, Brad, and Sam to be my supporters. I was surprised and hurt by their answer.

"We can't do it, Linda," Matt told me sadly.

"The guys in our bunk would think we were traitors if we went to the contest as your supporters," said Brad.

52

"But we will go as judges, to make sure the contest is fair," Sam tried to assure me.

"And we'll be rooting for you inside," said Matt.

I could see the boys' point. They didn't want to take teasing from the rest of their bunk. I didn't blame them, but I still felt awful. Without the boys there was no one to back me up. I was alone.

Help came from an unexpected source. I was sitting on my bed, tightening my sneakers in preparation for the big event, when Farah, Heather, and Rachel came by.

"The Bathroom Brigade, minus you, of course, just had a little meeting, Linda," said Farah. "We decided we want to go to the contest as your supporters."

"You do?" I looked at them in amazement. "But—but you know what that means, don't you? If we get caught, you'll get in trouble, too. Brenda Roman or one of her friends might decide to tell on us."

"Those 'Glitter Girls' aren't going to tell on anyone," said Heather. "They couldn't resist the chance to play up to Jed, so they're coming to the contest as his supporters. If we get into trouble, they'll get into trouble, too."

So it was settled; the lines were drawn. In one corner was Jed Lalotta and the Glitter Girls. In the other corner was Linda Berman and the Bathroom Brigade. This was going to be quite a contest—and one I had to win!

The Glitter Girls were already under the trees when we got there. They were drooling over Jed as if he were some sort of movie star. "Here comes the Bathroom Brigade," sang out Brenda, hoping to disturb us.

I was already one step ahead of her. Before we left the bunkhouse, I had gotten some art supplies and made signs for the four of us. "Proud member of the Bathroom Brigade" was pinned to our shirts. As we marched toward the tree where they were waiting, we sang a little song Farah had composed:

> Bathroom Brigade, Bathroom Brigade,
> we're the BEST!
> B means better than the rest!
> E is for energy that we've got!
> S is for strength; we're really hot!
> T is for talent, through and through,
> Bathroom Brigade, Bathroom Brigade,
> we're going to get you!
> Yeah! Bathroom Brigade!

The Glitter Girls and Jed stared at us in amazement. Brenda shook her head. "I guess it takes all types," she commented.

"Yes, and this type is going to teach *your* type a thing or two," I said. I was ready to go. "Let's get this contest started!"

"We're waiting for the referees," said Jed. "Sam was going to come up with some kind of scoring system to make sure the contest is fair."

"And I did it, too," Sam announced as he, Brad, and Matt made their appearance. "Don't think it was easy coming up with a way to score a tree-climbing contest, either. You can see why people don't do this professionally."

"Professional tree-climbing contest," scoffed Brenda. "Leave it to Sam to come up with a dumb idea like that!"

Sam ignored her and began to explain his system. Jed and I were each to choose a tree to climb at the same time. The first one to reach the spot in the tree that was as high as he or she could comfortably climb would call out, "Top!" At that point whoever was higher would score two points. Then Sam would time one additional minute on his stopwatch, giving us a chance to climb still higher. At the end of that minute, whoever was highest would score three points. One point would be subtracted for each slip or fall. The one with the most points would be declared the winner.

Quickly I went over Sam's scoring system in my mind and planned my strategy. I would have to be fast, but careful, because slips could lose points. But most important was to wind up highest, so I needed to choose a tree with strong branches that went all the way up.

My eyes scanned the treetops, looking for the perfect tree. Some had good thick branches down low, but thinned out near the top. It was those last points that were most important.

"Come on, Linda. I've picked mine already."

I looked and saw Jed standing under a very desirable tree. Of course, he must have had his picked out before I even got there. Why hadn't I thought to come early? I could have kicked myself right there.

Then I spotted a tree that I thought might be right for me. It was so high it was impossible to see way up to the top, but the branches on the bottom were easy to reach, and thick ones seemed to go quite a way up. I would have to take the chance. I took a deep breath. "This is the one I want."

"Good, then we're ready," said Sam. "Brad, you go stand under Jed's tree with his supporters. Matt, you go stand under Linda's with hers. Make sure you note any slips or falls."

"You can fall on me any time you want to, Jed," said Brenda with a disgusting lovesick smile.

This remark was too much even for Jed. "Come off it, Brenda. Falling on you isn't what will win this contest. And win it is what I intend to do!"

"Of course you will." Brenda giggled. "I was only kidding."

"Enough of this fooling around," Sam interrupted. "We want to get this contest over and done with before any of the counselors get wind of it. Let's get started. Ready, everyone?" He looked from Jed to me.

"Ready," we both replied.

Sam gave the signal, and we were off. I grabbed on to the lowest branch and boosted myself up on it. I scrambled to a standing position from where I was able to reach the next level, and from there the next. I moved rapidly, but not so fast that I chanced a slip or a fall. I was making good progress, but I had no way of knowing whether it was good enough because the leaves were too thick for me to be able to see Jed. He was taller and stronger than I was. It was possible he might make it up his tree first.

"Top!" I heard him yell and shouts arose from the crowd of kids below. I stopped where I was. I was way up in my tree, but I knew I could go higher. If Jed had reached his maximum, he had to have made it higher than I did.

"First round, no slips, Jed is the highest," Sam's voice called out. "Two points to Jed Lalotta."

The Glitter Girls let out cheers of joy. I felt this sick feeling in the pit of my stomach. I would never get over the humiliation if I lost this contest, never.

"Why take the chance of hurting yourself, Linda? You may as well quit now," Jed called to me.

I looked in his direction and found that the branches had thinned out enough so I could see him. He was higher than I was, but it couldn't have been by more than a few feet. I still had more rows of sturdy branches ahead of me, and he probably didn't. At this high level my smaller size and weight would be an advantage. There were still three points left. If I didn't slip, I had a chance to win this contest.

"I have no intention of quitting anything, Jed," I told him. "This contest isn't over yet!"

"Ready for the second part?" Sam yelled up to us. "Remember, you each have one minute to see if you can make any more progress. The one who's highest at the end of that time scores three points."

"That's going to be me," I told myself. As Sam called out, "Go!" I took off as fast as I could.

I guess I must have been a bit overeager. At any rate, I was climbing so quickly that I failed to notice a rotten area on the branch I was reaching for. The branch gave way; I slipped and had to grab on to the

57

one I was standing on to keep from falling to the ground.

"Slip! Minus one for Linda!" Matt called out.

The pain in my stomach intensified. Minus one. Now, even if I managed to climb up higher than Jed, the best I could do was tie him. Still, I was determined to keep on going. I slowed my pace a bit so I wouldn't make any more mistakes.

I dared to look over at Jed. He had no more thick branches left. I was higher than he was already; if he quit now, the contest would be a draw.

He looked at me and bit down on his lip. I could see he wasn't going to be satisfied with a tie. He reached for a branch that was way too small to hold his weight and tried to pull himself up on it.

"No, Jed, don't!" I tried to warn him, but Jed didn't listen.

Crack! The branch broke off from the tree, and Jed went down with it. The girls on the ground started to scream. It was a tense moment until Jed managed to grab the branch beneath him and prevent a nasty fall.

"Slip! Minus one for Jed!" Brad sang out.

"One minute's up! Three points for Linda!" called out Sam. "Final score, one point for Jed and two for Linda. Linda Berman's the official winner of the tree-climbing contest!"

"Yeah, Linda! Yeah, Linda!" Cheers went up from my supporters as I scrambled down my tree.

I didn't have time to enjoy my glory. As I neared the ground, I happened to look around. Good thing I did, because there, in the distance, I spotted Mr. Hawkins. He was making his way across the ballfield and heading straight for our group under the trees.

"Hawkins is coming! Hawkins is coming! Everyone back to the bunks!" I called out.

Everyone scattered, and Jed and I managed to swing out of our trees and take off through the woods before Hawkins reached us.

"Hey, you two! Stop! I want to talk to you!" he called out.

Jed and I had no intention of stopping. We darted through the trees, then circled through the woods. We made it back to our bunks just in time for evening activity.

I didn't think Hawkins had recognized who we were since he hadn't called us by name. Finally it looked as if I might have gotten away with something!

Chapter
Nine

After the tree-climbing contest, word spread through camp of my victory, and kids regarded me with new respect. Jed seemed to respect me more as well, because he made no more attempts to show me up. Maybe he came to see that co-ed sports weren't so terrible after all.

The new setup actually brought some advantages for the boys. Before, bunk 9 usually played against bunk 10, and since bunk 10 boys were a year older, bunk 9 almost always lost. With the new system of merging teams of boys and girls of the same age, the rival red and blue teams were set up to be pretty equally matched. That meant that anyone could win, and there was almost always a good game.

Co-ed sports seemed to make everyone try harder. Even girls like Brenda, Sharon, and Melissa had to pay attention to the game or risk the embarrassment of looking bad in front of the boys.

As the days passed, it became more and more evident that the Glitter Girls were using the sports period to try to play up to the boys they thought were the cutest. Sharon and Melissa were always hanging around Sam and Brad, doing silly things like throwing balls at them or making dumb remarks.

Brad and Sam were far too smart to get sucked into this. They made a point of ignoring Sharon and Melissa until the girls finally gave up.

Brenda, however, was having better results. She liked Jed, and for some reason he seemed to enjoy having her fuss over him.

I guess it was the fact that Jed was the captain of the red team that made Brenda take a sudden interest in sports. She had never cared enough about playing ball before to learn to do it properly. Now she took the game seriously, and it really was funny to see.

It didn't take long for Brenda to push things too far. She had made a few lucky catches, which made her think she was a real ballplayer. Then she convinced Jed to let her play an important position. Instead of putting her in the outfield, where she belonged, Jed actually let Brenda play second base.

"Oh, no, Jed! How could you?" the boys on the red team groaned.

But Jed didn't listen to them. "Brenda's been playing really well. She deserves a shot at the infield," he insisted.

I couldn't wait to take advantage of the fact that Brenda was playing second. My chance came in the eighth inning, when our teams were tied three-all.

There were two outs when it was my turn to bat. I took aim and swung my hardest.

Whack! The bat connected with the ball, sending it right toward Brenda. It wasn't a hard catch to make, but luckily for me, she missed it as if there were a hole in her glove. I made it to first base.

"Oh, no!" the kids on the red team called out in disappointment. "That was an easy catch, Brenda! You should have had it!"

Brenda's face went red with embarrassment. She knew she had blown an easy one.

"Come on, Brenda! You can get her out when she runs to second!" Jed tried to encourage her. Having Brenda blow that play didn't make his judgment look very good.

"Don't worry! She'll never get by me!" Brenda bragged.

Of course, that only made me even more determined to get by her no matter what. Matt was up at bat after me. He was a good hitter, but he usually hit singles, which wouldn't be enough to let me make it all the way home. Heather was up after Matt, and she wasn't a very good hitter. If she made an out, the inning would be over without my having a chance to score.

That's when I came up with my daring plan. The only way for me to be sure to score was to steal second. That way I could make it home on Matt's single.

I waited to be sure the pitcher's gaze was fixed on the batter. As he prepared to release the ball, I took off running toward second as fast as I could.

Brenda started to scream as soon as she saw me coming. "Quick! Quick! Throw me the ball! Throw me the ball!"

I never saw the ball coming, but I did see Brenda. She stood right in my path to second base.

I darted to the right to try to get around her. She moved right in an attempt to block me.

I dived to the ground, sliding to the base. Brenda tripped over my feet. She wound up sprawling in the dirt and losing the ball.

"Safe!" Jeff, the umpire, called out.

With that this horrible wail arose from Brenda. "My ankle! My ankle! She broke my ankle, and she did it on purpose!"

Everyone came rushing over to see Brenda's injuries. She was crying and carrying on and claiming she couldn't walk, so we all had to wait for a stretcher to be sent for to take her to the infirmary. By that time it was too late to finish the game, which I knew our team would have won.

Brenda's ankle was only twisted, not broken. That didn't stop her from playing the situation for all it was worth. She returned from the infirmary bandaged up and leaning on crutches. She got out of her job serving and cleaning for two whole days. She had Sharon and Melissa, and even Aileen and Carol, waiting on her hand and foot. And she kept telling everyone who would listen that I had tripped her on purpose to keep her from catching the ball, so the accident was my fault.

This was typical of Brenda—trying to make herself look good by making me look bad. It really got me angry, but it was nothing compared to what she did with Farah's swimming lessons.

It was more difficult than I thought it would be to teach Farah to swim. For one thing, it meant I had to give up my free swim period in order to have time to work with her. I wouldn't have minded that so much if she hadn't been so tough to work with.

It probably wouldn't have been so bad if I didn't have to work with Farah after her group swimming session with Scott. There were so many kids in Beginner Swim that Scott didn't have much time to work with them individually. He tried to get them to lose their fear of water by having them go under and come back up again so they would see that water wouldn't hurt them.

This approach worked for most of the kids, but not for Farah. She put up a fight, kicking and screaming. She absolutely refused to put her head under water. By the time I got to her, she was shivering with fear.

"You've got to relax, Farah," was the first thing I told her.

"I know—b-but I can't!" she said. "Don't even try to make me go under water, Linda!"

"I won't," I promised. But I didn't know what else to do. If Scott, who was a trained swimming instructor, couldn't help Farah, how could I?

Then I had an idea. "I think the first thing you have to do, Farah, is to see how easy it is to float. The water pushes you up naturally when you're relaxed, the way it does to a beach ball or a raft."

"That's what Scott says, but I don't believe it."

"Well, I'm going to prove it to you," I told her. "I'm going to do a dead man's float here in the water. I'll lie here with my arms and legs stretched out and my face down. I want you to put your hand on my back and try to push me under."

"I don't want to push you under, Linda, you could drown!" Farah was horrified at the idea.

"I'm not going to be under that long, silly! I just want you to push me down enough to feel the resistance from the water. Then stop pushing and leave your hand on my back to feel how the water pushes me back up again."

"Okay," Farah said doubtfully. I went into a float, and she did as I had asked.

"Wow! That's wild!" Farah was giggling when I came up for air. "I really could feel the water pushing you up! I really could!"

That example seemed to help Farah lose some fear of the water. I was able to get her to hold on to the edge of the dock and kick her legs in the water. That at least gave her the feeling of swimming. It took a few days of doing this before she felt confident enough to let go of the dock and hold on to my hands. Then I led her around the shallow part of the lake.

All the while I was busy with Farah, Brenda was using the free swim period to show off with her daring dives and super strokes. But after her ankle had healed enough for her to return to regular camp activities, this was no longer enough for Brenda. She discovered free-swim period was a perfect time to get to me.

The first day she was back, she didn't go into the

water. She sat on the edge of the dock making dumb comments. "How can you let Linda lead you around like that, Farah? I wouldn't trust her if I were you. She could let go of you at any time!"

"Don't listen to a word she's saying," I assured Farah. But I could feel her body stiffen with tension, and the lesson was ruined for the day.

But that wasn't enough for Brenda. The next day she swam under the ropes and made her way to the shallow water without being spotted. I was holding Farah's hands while she kicked in the water, as usual. I was concentrating on Farah so hard that I never saw Brenda until she grabbed on to my feet underwater.

"Shark attack! Shark attack!" she screamed as she came splashing to the surface.

Brenda really got me by surprise that time. I was so startled that I let go of Farah's hands and stepped back. I whirled around to face my attacker.

"You creep!" I said angrily when I saw that it was Brenda. But she was already swimming back to the deep water. And then I remembered about Farah. I had let go of her hands. Now she would never trust me again!

Before I could turn around, someone grabbed me around my waist. It was Farah, using my body to pull herself to the surface. I couldn't believe it. She had managed to swim the few feet to me all by herself!

"I did it, Linda! I did it!" Farah was laughing as she stood up triumphantly. "I swam without holding on to anyone!"

"Wow, Farah, that was great!" I said happily.

"Brenda's plan really backfired this time. Here she was trying her hardest to ruin your swimming lessons, and she turned out being the reason you learned how to swim!"

Chapter
Ten

After that things began to look better for me at camp. I started to think that if it weren't for Brenda, I might actually like it.

Farah was making real progress with her swimming lessons, which made me feel proud. The Bathroom Brigade finally finished our bathroom duty. Our next assignment was general bunk cleaning, which was a lot more pleasant than cleaning toilets and sinks. And it was now the Glitter Girls' turn to have bathroom duty, which did my heart good to see.

An event was coming up that I was really looking forward to. This was our first overnight camp-out. Our bunk was going to spend a night in the woods!

"We don't want to sleep out in the woods," protested Brenda. "What if it rains? What if some bug or lizard or wild animal attacks us? Why do we have to have a camp-out? This is my fourth year at Camp Winnepeg, and we never had to do this before!"

"That's because you were too young before," said Aileen. "Going on an overnight is a privilege. Campers don't get to do it until they're at least ten."

"Well, consider me nine, then," Brenda pouted. "I can't sleep on hard, rocky soil. I refuse to go. And if I don't go, Sharon and Melissa won't, either."

"Yeah, we won't, either," echoed Melissa.

"And if you try to make us, we'll complain to Mr. Hawkins," added Sharon.

"Well, I'm sorry to hear you say that, girls," Aileen said. "Because I know the boys in bunk 9 will be disappointed if you decide not to go. You see, they're scheduled to go on the camp-out with us."

Brenda, Sharon, and Melissa exchanged looks. "The boys in bunk 9 will be coming with us?" repeated Brenda. "Does that include Jed Lalotta?"

"That's right." Aileen smiled. "When I spoke to Greg about it, he said the boys in his group were really eager to go."

"Well, in that case, it probably would be okay after all," said Brenda. "Don't you think so, girls?"

Sharon and Melissa nodded their agreement. "Yeah, we don't want to disappoint the boys," they said.

It made me sick to listen to them. I didn't know why Aileen had to convince the Glitter Girls to come on the hike. Who needed them there, anyhow?

We spent a good part of the afternoon getting ready for the camp-out. We had to pack up our clothes for the next day and our bedding, and roll it up in such a way that we could carry it in our backpacks. We had to carry food to cook for dinner and enough for breakfast, too.

"This is way too heavy for me to carry," Brenda griped as Carol added some cooking utensils to the load she was carrying. "You can't expect me to actually hike through the woods with all this on my back!"

"Stop complaining, Brenda," Carol replied. "You're not carrying more than anyone else is."

"Well, if I suffer from exhaustion because of this activity, Mr. Hawkins will hear about it immediately," Brenda threatened.

"Fine, Brenda." Carol let out a deep sigh. "And since Mr. Hawkins is the one who okayed this hike in the first place, I'm sure he'll be happy to discuss it with you. Now, get going and stop complaining."

"Looks like even Carol is losing patience with Brenda," Farah commented to me as we set off on the path that led through the woods.

"If I had my way, everyone in Camp Winnepeg would know how disgusting Brenda is," I told her.

"Well, if anyone can find a way to do that, it's got to be you," she said.

The thought of Brenda's being humiliated in front of the entire camp kept me going on the long hike through the woods to our campsite. The afternoon was hot, and my backpack grew very heavy as we climbed up the hill that led deeper into the woods. I found myself hoping we would get there soon before I would have to embarrass myself by asking to stop for a rest.

"Here's the clearing!" Aileen's voice finally rang out

as I neared the point where I didn't think I could take another step.

"It's about time!" Brenda plopped wearily down on the ground, easing her backpack off her shoulders. The other girls followed her lead. I was about to do the same when I heard loud noises coming through the trees.

Sharon jumped up from where she was standing and grabbed on to Melissa. "Ooh! What's that?" she asked nervously.

"Maybe it's a w-wild animal." Melissa was practically shaking.

For a moment I was frightened, too. I knew kids had come across deer and raccoons, which were harmless enough. But what if there was something more dangerous in the woods, like a bear or a wolf?

Then I spotted a flash of red material that no animal could possibly be wearing. "It's the boys! They must have gotten here before us!" I called out. Forgetting how tired I was, I dropped my backpack and went plunging ahead to meet them.

"Hi, guys! What are you up to?" I asked as I reached Matt and Sam. The two of them were struggling to carry an armload of sticks and tree branches.

"We're gathering wood to build our lean-tos," said Brad. He was effortlessly dragging a load by himself.

"A lean-to? What's a lean-to?" asked Farah, who had followed me.

"That's a lean-to." Brad pointed to a flimsy structure of twigs and sticks that was propped up against a tree. "Jeff and Greg showed us how to build one, and now we're making our own."

"You girls had better get your own lean-tos started if you want to have something to sleep under tonight," suggested Sam. "It's pretty easy to make—all you've got to do is build a frame with the long sticks. Then you weave the small branches across the frame. If you do it right, the lean-to will give some protection from wind and rain."

"What? A bunch of twigs and sticks are no protection from wind and rain!" Brenda came over and stuck in her two cents' worth. "I need a real roof."

"Well, you're not going to find one out here in the woods." Matt seemed very happy to inform her.

"Aileen!" Brenda let out a wail. "The boys are only kidding, aren't they? You don't expect us to sleep here with nothing but these lean-tos as shelter, do you?"

"But of course, Brenda," Aileen answered. "This is a camp-out, not Cinderella's ball. You did know we were going to rough it, didn't you?"

"Roughing it is one thing," replied Brenda. "Sleeping under sticks is something else. I can't sleep under conditions like this."

"Then I guess you'll have to stay up all night," Aileen said. "And I hate to be the one to inform you, but there are no flush toilets in the woods, either."

"No flush toilets!" Brenda was shrieking now. "Why, that's absolutely, positively uncivilized!"

"Perhaps," said Aileen. "But I'm afraid you'll have to deal with it like everyone else does."

We all burst out laughing at the look of horror on Brenda's face. It was worth having no flush toilets to see Brenda so flustered. But even I didn't think it would be too great to have to sleep in a flimsy lean-to if it started to rain. I sure hoped the weather would hold out until morning!

Luck was with us. The night was crisp and clear, with no rain clouds in sight. Greg and Jeff showed us how to build a campfire and to cut sticks of green wood on which to roast our hotdogs. They were the best hotdogs I ever tasted.

We cleaned up after dinner, then everyone sat around the campfire. Carol, whose brother was a ranger at a national park, talked to us about the beauty and balance of nature.

"Every plant we saw today, every animal and tiny insect, has a special part to play in the particular natural habitat we have in this area," she said. "Once Native Americans roamed these woods, living in harmony with the rest of nature. Then came the Europeans, with our advanced civilization, and the balance changed. The forests were cleared; the animals were killed or disappeared because they no longer had a place to find food and make their homes. Wall to wall cities now fill much of the eastern coast, spewing pollution into the environment."

Carol gazed around the circle as she spoke. All eyes were solemnly fixed upon her. I wondered if everyone else felt as sad as I did at the loss of the beautiful forests and the wildlife that had lived there.

"But here, in Camp Winnepeg, we are lucky to have a little piece of nature preserved for us," she continued. "I hope each one of you can appreciate the wonders of this special place enough to want to do your part in protecting the environment. Let's start by making sure that before we leave here, we pitch in to clean up after ourselves and leave things as we found them. That way nature is not disturbed, and this beauty can continue for others to enjoy."

When Carol finished, everyone was silent for a moment. I tried to imagine what it must have been like a few hundred years ago when the country was covered with forests and animals, and Native Americans lived on this very spot.

Surprisingly, it wasn't hard to do. Here in the forest, basking in the light of the fire, gazing up through the break in the trees at the star-studded sky, I felt that I, too, was a part of nature. I and the trees and the stars and the animals— there was something that connected us. I didn't know what it was, but I felt it so strongly I knew it was really there.

"Okay, guys. Enough of this serious stuff—how about some camp songs?" Greg broke the mood by saying. He got out his guitar, and we all began to sing. I don't know if it was the leftover feeling from Carol's talk or the singing that did it, but I felt very close to everyone as we sat around the fire. I didn't even have a negative thought about Brenda Roman until we started, "If I Had a Hammer." Then I couldn't help glancing over to where she was sitting to see what she was up to.

It was at that moment that Brenda got up from her place by the fire. I saw her exchange strange glances with Jed, then head off on the path that led through the woods to the outhouse. But right before she disappeared into the darkness, I saw her take a sharp turn off the path.

Why would she do that? Brenda wasn't the type to

go wandering off into the woods at night. Maybe I should follow her and see what she's up to, I thought. Then I thought better of it. After all, I wasn't wild about the thought of walking through the woods in the dark. Maybe, with a little luck, Brenda might get lost and stay lost.

As I was enjoying this thought, I noticed Jed rise to his feet. I watched him head down the path to the outhouse. After glancing back, he went off into the woods right where Brenda had.

Why, he must be going to meet Brenda, I realized. I was dying to know what the two of them might be doing. "Brenda and Jed just disappeared into the woods together," I whispered to Matt, who was sitting next to me. "Want to go see what they're up to?"

He grinned. "That could prove to be lots of fun."

"Good," I said. "I'm going to have Farah come with me into the woods. We'll find the turnoff to the left and wait for you there. Tell Brad and Sam what's going on, wait a few minutes, then come meet us."

It wasn't very hard to find them. To the left of the path was a clump of bushes, and behind it was a small clearing where Brenda and Jed must have figured they'd be safe from prying eyes. Ordinarily they would have been—no one would have thought to look for them there if I hadn't seen them head off the path. And I guess there was so much noise coming from around the campfire, where the rest of our group was still singing away, that Brenda and Jed didn't hear us approaching.

There they stood, clearly outlined by the moonlight. Their arms were wrapped around each other, and

75

their faces drew close together in preparation for a kiss.

Covering our mouths to keep from laughing, the rest of us crowded around to get a better view. "Oh, Jed, you're so cute!" Brenda murmured.

That did it. No one could control themselves after that remark. We all burst out in peals of laughter. Then I led our group in a chorus of that famous taunt, "Jed and Brenda sitting in a tree, K-I-S-S-I-N-G!"

Jed and Brenda pulled apart, a look of horror on their faces as they became aware of the audience gathered around them.

"You—you creepy little sneaks!" Brenda sputtered. "This is all your fault, Linda, I know it is! But you're not going to get away with embarrassing me this time! Wait till I find some way to get even with you!"

I didn't take her very seriously. After all, as far as I was concerned, Brenda and I were already in a state of total war.

Chapter
Eleven

For the next few days I watched Brenda very carefully for signs of any plots to get me. Once I caught her trying to slip something out of the cabinet where I kept my personal things.

"Thief! Thief! Brenda's a thief!" I put up such a fuss that everyone in the bunk stared at Brenda. Carol came over to give her a speech about respecting other people's property.

After that I was sure Brenda wouldn't dare try stealing from me again. But getting caught like that made her resent me even more. She lost no opportunity to make a nasty remark or to try to embarrass me or make me look bad. I knew it was just a matter of time before she made some major attempt to get me.

I kept a watchful eye on Brenda, but mostly I was busy getting ready for the next big event at camp that was fast approaching. The coming Sunday was Parents' Visiting Day at Camp Winnepeg. All parents and brothers and sisters were invited to come see what camp was like.

"Naturally, we want Camp Winnepeg to be at its best on visiting day," Mr. Hawkins announced to the entire camp as we gathered in front of the dining hall. "I expect everyone to pitch in and clean up the grounds and the bunkhouses. We'll have displays of your arts and crafts projects and demonstrations of different sports activities and swimming."

"Swimming!" Farah whispered to me in horror. "There's no way I'm going to have anything to do with that!"

"Don't worry about it," I assured her. "You've been doing great recently. I promise to work with you even harder until Parents' Day.

"And finally, we'll put on a little show for the parents," Mr. Hawkins went on. "I want each bunk to prepare a skit to perform. Nothing big or fancy, just something to show some typical camp activity that you particularly enjoy. Discuss it with your bunk, and see what you come up with. Remember, the image of Camp Winnepeg depends on you!"

For a change our bunk had no trouble coming up with an idea. With the exception of Brenda, everyone agreed that our night sleeping out in the forest was the best time we had had at camp. We came up with a skit about our hike through the forest and showing how we built a lean-to. The boys of bunk 9 wanted to do their skit about how to build a campfire. We decided to combine our skits and end them with both bunks sitting around the campfire, talking about how important it was to take good care of our environment, and then singing our Camp Winnepeg song.

"That's a lousy ending," protested Brenda. "Everyone will think we're lecturing them about taking care of the environment."

"We won't be lecturing, we'll be informing," I told her. "Unless, of course, you and Jed would like to end it with a demonstration of other things that can go on in the woods!"

"Shut up, Linda!" Brenda glared at me as everyone burst out laughing.

Parents' Visiting Day dawned bright and sunny. Everyone got up early and set to work getting the bunkhouse extra clean.

"Boy, am I glad this is our last day on bathroom duty," I overheard Melissa say to Brenda as I passed the entrance to the bathroom. "Next week all we have to do is general cleaning, which, after this, will seem like a piece of cake."

"I know," Brenda answered. "And you know what, it's almost impossible to tell if we're doing a good job with general cleaning. We can take it real easy, and no one will be the wiser."

"I will." I stuck my head into the bathroom and grinned at them.

"Oh, you!" Brenda screwed up her face in anger when she saw me. "You're always interfering with my life, Linda. You've made this the most miserable time in camp I've ever had!"

"I'm sorry to hear that, Brenda," I said with a tone

79

of mock sadness. "Because I'm finding I'm enjoying camp a lot more than I ever thought I would!"

Brenda and I might have had a fight right then, but we were interrupted by an announcement on the camp public address system.

"Attention, boys and girls!" Mr. Hawkins's voice came through. "Parents' Visiting Day has officially begun with the arrival of the first carload of visitors. As your parents arrive, I'll call for you over the loudspeaker. Please come meet your parents at the dining hall when you hear your name."

Everyone strained to hear whose name would be first. I should have known who it would be. "Brenda Roman!"

"I knew it! I knew it!" Brenda jumped up and down. "My parents are always *dying* to see me."

"And seeing her probably makes them want to die!" I muttered to Farah.

"What was that you said about me, Linda?" Brenda demanded angrily.

I was about to tell her when Mr. Hawkins's voice was heard again. "Attention, boys and girls! It seems I overlooked the fact that two sets of parents arrived in that very first car. Linda Berman, come to the dining room with Brenda. Your parents came up together with hers!"

Brenda and I looked at each other. Our parents had arrived in the same car together. What if that meant they expected us all to spend the day together? That would be awful!

Ordinarily, Brenda and I would have walked to the

80

dining room far apart, without looking at or talking to each other. This morning, however, we walked together. We were deep in conversation as to what was the best way to handle this situation.

"My parents think everything is wonderful for me up here in camp," Brenda admitted. "And I don't want anything to ruin that—least of all you! Do you understand what I'm saying?"

"That you don't want them to know about the state of war that exists between us. That you want them to think you're Miss Popularity here at camp."

"Well, I would be if it weren't for you!" Brenda glared at me. Then her face softened into the phoniest-looking smile. "Look, Linda, do me this favor and pretend we're getting along okay. It'll only be for a minute. I'll get my parents away from yours right away. How about it?"

I pretended to be weighing this carefully in my mind. Actually, I was very happy with Brenda's suggestion. I didn't want my parents to know I was involved in this feud with Brenda, either. But I wasn't about to give Brenda the satisfaction of letting her know that. "What's in it for me if I go along with your plan?" I bargained.

"It's just like you to take advantage, isn't it, Linda?" Brenda screwed her face into an ugly pout. "But to show you how big I am, I'll make a deal with you. You pretend everything's fine between us, and I won't say a nasty thing to you all day. Not only that, I'll forget that I still owe you one over what you did to embarrass me at the camp-out. You'll be off the hook!"

"Off the hook—ha! Don't think for one moment that I was ever worried about anything you might do, Brenda. But you happen to have caught me in a generous mood. I'll do you the favor and agree to your little scheme. Pretend we're best of friends, if it makes you happy."

I had to laugh to myself as Brenda and I approached the dining room. She would have kicked herself if only she knew that I had been about to suggest to her that we pretend to be getting along in front of our parents, too. If Brenda had played it smart, she wouldn't have had to offer me any kind of deal.

"There's Linda! Linda!" The voices of my six-year-old twin brothers, Ira and Joey, rang out in stereophonic sound. They ran up to me, and before I realized what was happening, I was hugging them. I couldn't believe how glad I was to see my pesty brothers after having been away from them for so long.

Then my Mom and Dad were there, and I was hugging them. I was so happy to have my family with me.

"Let me have a look at you!" My mother held me at arm's length when we got through with all that hugging. "I think you lost some weight. Are you sure you're eating enough here? And whatever happened to your *hair?*"

Her voice went up an octave when she said that, and I raised my hand to feel my scraggly hair, which was beginning to grow back. Everyone at camp was used to seeing me with short hair, and I was used to myself that way. I had forgotten that my parents had never seen my haircut.

"Oh—uh—my hair! Well, I—uh—thought it would be easier to take care of short at camp. It's—uh—faster to dry after swimming, and I—uh—don't have to fuss with it this way." I glanced in Brenda's direction when I said this. She was examining some new outfits her parents had brought her. I could tell she was dying to say something about the real reason I had cut my hair, but she didn't dare.

"Oh. Well, I guess it will grow back before too long." My mother was a good sport about it. "And now, how about showing us all around camp?"

"Sure, let's go right away," I said, relieved to escape from Brenda so quickly. "See you later, Brenda."

"Not so fast." Mr. Roman's booming voice stopped us from leaving. "We told your parents we would all tour Camp Winnepeg together, Linda. After all, we've been involved for so long that we can give them much more information."

"Oh." I didn't know what to say to Mr. Roman. He reminded me of an army drill sergeant who was used to giving orders and having things his way. Desperately I looked to Brenda. Could she come up with something to save this situation?

Brenda grabbed her father's hand and gazed up at him adoringly. "Oh, Daddy, that was so nice of you, but I'm afraid it wouldn't work for us to all go around camp together. We would be far too large a group to go in and out of the buildings easily. Besides, I have some special things I wanted to show you in private. It would be better for everyone if we toured camp separately, really it would."

"Well, uh . . ." Mr. Roman looked embarrassed. "It depends on how the Bermans feel about it."

"Oh, don't worry about our getting to see enough, George," my mother was quick to say. "I'm sure Linda knows what to show us, and we can still meet for lunch the way we originally planned."

"Lunch?" Brenda and I asked together.

"Yes, we have a special treat for you girls," Mrs. Roman said with a wide smile. "No camp food for you today. We've packed up a picnic lunch of sandwiches, salads, fruit, and your favorite chocolate cake, Brenda. Why don't we all meet right here just before noon so we can enjoy it together?"

Before Brenda or I could get a word in, these plans were agreed to by our parents. The two of us looked at each other. The thought of having to have lunch together, putting on a show for our parents the whole time, was overwhelmingly awful.

Lunch with Brenda was every bit as bad as I thought it would be. My parents were busy talking to Brenda's parents. My brothers finished lunch and ran off to chase butterflies. Brenda and I were stuck sitting there together with the next to impossible task of trying to have a conversation that wouldn't end in a fight.

"Uh—this is great chocolate cake your mother brought, Brenda," I attempted as I cut myself another slice.

"Well, don't be such a pig and hog it all!" she snapped irritably.

84

"It's only my second piece," I told her. "Are you upset because you're too fat to have seconds?"

"I am not fat! I just know enough to watch my calories. I couldn't eat another thing around you, anyhow—watching you eat is enough to make me lose my appetite! Didn't anyone ever teach you table manners?"

"I have fine table manners—when I want to, Brenda!" Deliberately I licked some chocolate off my fingers. "It's just that the cake tastes so-oo much better when you eat it this way. Here, try some!"

"Yuck!" Brenda jumped up as I held my sticky fingers out to her.

"What's the matter, girls?" Mrs. Roman interrupted her conversation with my mother to ask.

"Oh, nothing, Mother," Brenda said quickly. "I just noticed some ants crawling near the food."

"Leave it to ants to ruin a picnic!" Mrs. Roman said. "Well, I guess we ought to be cleaning up now, anyway, since everyone seems to have had enough to eat."

"Good idea." My mother began gathering up the plastic food containers and snapping on the lids. "Linda, will you do me a favor and go get your brothers? I see they've run off way down the meadow."

Ordinarily I hated to run after my brothers, but now I agreed right away. Anything to get away from Brenda.

"You can go with Linda if you like, Brenda," Mrs. Roman said.

"Oh, no, Mother. I'd be more useful helping you

85

clean up. Here, let me get that chocolate cake and wrap it up before some animal gets to it!" Brenda looked straight at me when she said that. I knew exactly what she meant, but I wouldn't give her the satisfaction of a response.

I went off to get my brothers, grateful that this picnic had finally come to an end.

The major events of Parents' Visiting Day were planned for the afternoon. First there was a swimming exhibition, and then would be our camp show.

My parents and the Romans insisted on sitting together during the swimming exhibition. At least Brenda and I didn't have to sit with them the whole time, since we were taking part in the show.

My group, Intermediate Swim, went first. We had a relay race in which everyone had to swim two laps while holding on to a spoon to hand off to the next person on the team. My team didn't win, but I still felt good about my effort.

"Why, Linda, we're so pleased to see how much better you're swimming than when you first started camp," my mother said when I returned to sit with my family after my group was finished.

"Can you teach us to swim like that?" my brothers asked.

I felt really proud of my achievements until it was time for Advanced Swim, Brenda's group, to perform. They demonstrated fancy dives and lifesaving skills. Then the girls put on a water ballet in which they swam into formations that looked like stars and flowers. Their performance made our relay race look like nothing. Worst of all, Brenda was the star of the show.

"Brenda, that was wonderful!" "You really looked professional out there." "What a strong stroke you have!" "What grace!" "What skill!" Compliments rained on Brenda as she returned to where we were sitting. I felt like throwing up right there. To make matters worse, my parents were giving more praise to her than they had to me.

What was so great about what Brenda had done, anyway? Didn't my parents realize that Brenda had had private swimming lessons, that she was already an expert swimmer before coming to camp, that I had made more progress this summer than she had? Didn't they remember that I was their daughter?

"And now, last but not least—our Beginner Swim," Mr. Hawkins announced. "These kids may not have fancy strokes or dives to show you, but keep in mind that they didn't swim at all when they first came to Camp Winnepeg. And look what they can do now!"

The Beginner Group started their show. It really wasn't much. The group stood in a big circle. As Scott, the swimming counselor, blew his whistle, the kids put their faces in the water and floated while kicking their feet. Then some of them began to really swim. A few made it across an entire lap.

There was a scattering of polite applause for the beginners. I got up and cheered as loudly as I could. After all, Farah was one of those who swam the whole lap. I had worked with her long and hard to get her to finally start to swim. I knew how much it meant to her.

"What are you making such a fuss about, anyhow, Linda?" Brenda demanded. "What they're doing is worthless."

At her words I felt hot anger rush to my head. I forgot my promise to get along with Brenda in front of our parents. She always had to prove she was so great in front of everyone. What she needed was to be taught a lesson.

Then it came to me. Our skit—that was the moment I could give it to Brenda. I would wait until our group was up on the stage, finishing the singing of our camp song. Then I would make the announcement that there were certain people who had discovered the perfect way to end a campfire. I would let the entire camp and the parents know that Brenda Roman and Jed Lalotta were caught kissing in the woods!

"That shows how little you know, Brenda," I began. But before I had a chance to say anything else, Farah, still dripping water from the lake, came running over to me.

"Linda! Linda! I have to introduce you to my parents! I told them how you took time from your own swim period every day to teach me to swim. Mom, Dad, this is Linda, my very best friend here at camp. She's the greatest!"

I felt myself blushing as Farah's parents thanked me for doing so much for her. Then they went over to tell my parents how kind and caring they thought I was.

My parents beamed. Brenda's moment of glory was quickly forgotten. I felt wonderful.

It was the strangest thing. The good feelings that I got from being appreciated by Farah and her parents stayed with me for a long time. They stayed with me while the other bunks put on their skits. They stayed with me while our bunk got up on the stage and built our lean-to. They stayed with me while we gathered around the campfire bunk 9 built, gave our talk about the environment, and began our camp song:

Here's to you, our Camp Winnepeg.
We salute you with our song.
Swimming, hiking, art, and sports,
It's fun the whole day long.
But the things we hold most dear
Are the friendships we make that last all year.
We can't wait to come back here
And be together again, singing:
Here's to you, our Camp Winnepeg.
We salute you with our song!

The song ended. We all stood up in our circle, grasping the hands of the person on either side of us. I felt so close to everyone. I didn't want anything to break the mood.

That's when I remembered my plot to get even with Brenda. This was the point in the program where I had planned to make the announcement, to tell the whole camp about another activity for camp-outs, one that Brenda and Jed had introduced us to—kissing in the forest. This was the moment I had been waiting for—my moment of triumph.

But then I thought back to other moments of triumph in my feud with Brenda, those other times when I had scored points against her. I would feel good, but it would only last a moment. After the moment wore off, I would wind up feeling bad again. I really didn't like being at war.

That's when I realized that if I did say something about Brenda, my good feelings were going to immediately disappear. Was it worth the trade-off—my moment of triumph versus the glow of peace and friendship I was experiencing now?

I decided it wasn't. For this night, at least, I would keep the peace.

Chapter
Twelve

For a few days there was an uneasy peace between Brenda and me. I made up my mind I wasn't going to be the one to break it.

Brenda, of course, couldn't last very long without making some sort of attempt to get to me. This time her attempt was a feeble one. She actually thought she would scare me by planting a lizard under the covers of my bed.

I knew Brenda was behind it because she, Sharon, and Melissa all "happened" to be standing around my bed as I slipped in under the covers. When I called out, "Yuck! There's something *alive* in my bed with me!" they began to laugh as if this were the funniest thing in the world.

As soon as I realized the Glitter Girls were up to something, I pulled myself together. I refused to act frightened and peered under the covers to see what was there.

What I saw was this tiny red creature, hardly bigger than my middle finger. It stared at me through frightened eyes. I picked it up and held it in my hand. Its throat moved up and down with every breath. I could feel its heart beating rapidly.

"This poor thing is scared to death," I announced. "I wonder what kind of mean, miserable excuse for a human being could have put it here?"

I glared right at Brenda when I said this.

"Don't look at me!" she said. "You wouldn't catch me touching anything slimy like that!"

While that was probably true, I still knew that Brenda was behind it somehow. I wouldn't be at all surprised if she had snuck Jed into our bunk to put this lizard in my bed.

I didn't have time to bother with Brenda now, however. Carol came over to see what was happening. I showed the lizard to her.

"Look what was in my bed. Carol. Isn't he the cutest thing? I want to keep him for a pet. Can I? Can I?"

Carol looked down at the creature in my hand. "Why, it's a salamander. You can find them sometimes in the woods around here. I wonder how he got into your bed?" She looked at Brenda when she said this. Brenda put on her expression of angelic innocence she uses to get away with everything.

Carol turned her attention back to me. "But where would you keep him, Linda? Salamanders have to be near water. We can't have him running around loose in the bunk."

I thought fast. "My art box!" Still carrying the salamander, I jumped off the bed and got the plastic container in which I had packed the art supplies I had brought to camp. I dumped everything into my camp bag. I placed the salamander in the container along with a little water and a pretty rock I had found outside.

"Tomorrow I'll get some dirt and moss and plants for him so he'll feel right at home," I promised. "Say I can keep him, Carol, please!"

"You'll have to catch little insects to feed him with, and you'll have to clean out that container all the time," said Carol.

"No problem. I'll take care of Sal, I promise!"

"So you've already named him!" Carol laughed. I knew I had won. "Well, I guess you can keep him then, Linda. But remember, he's your pet, and you're responsible for him."

"Great!" I took Sal and his container and placed him on the cabinet next to my bed.

"Ugh! We don't want to have to sleep in the same bunk as that lizard," Brenda protested.

"Then you might have been more careful not to let him get into Linda's bed," Carol said meaningfully. "Now go back to your own beds, girls. If you don't bother Sal, I'm sure he's not going to bother you!"

I grew attached to Sal very quickly. Every morning when I woke up, I went to check on him first thing. I would search for bugs to bring him to eat. I would hold him in my hand and take him outside and let him walk on the grass for exercise. I would check on him again before I went to sleep.

Having Sal made me kind of a celebrity around

camp. Whenever I was out with him, kids would gather around to watch him and ask to hold him and pet him. I enjoyed this a lot, especially since it was so obvious that Brenda was burning with jealousy and resentment over the attention I was getting. Her plot against me had really backfired this time.

The last week of camp arrived, and I realized I would be sorry when it ended. Now that I had made some friends, learned not to let Brenda get to me, and had Sal for a pet, I found I actually liked Camp Winnepeg.

Then came the morning I woke up and went to check on Sal as usual. I looked in his container but didn't see him. My heart began pounding as I searched through the moss and plants and under the rock I had put there for him. I couldn't find him anywhere!

"Help!" I called out desperately. "Sal's not in his container. He must be around the bunk somewhere. Will somebody help me find him?"

Except for the Glitter Girls, everyone in the bunk joined in the search for Sal. We looked inside of everything and behind everything and under and on top of everything, but there was no sign of my little salamander. Sal was gone!

I threw myself on my bed, overwhelmed by this terrible sense of loss. I couldn't believe how much Sal had come to mean to me in so short a time. I thought of the cute way he looked at me and the way his breathing would calm down when I rubbed his back. I felt so awful I wanted to bury myself under the covers and stay in bed.

"Time for breakfast, Linda." Carol's voice interrupted my misery.

"I don't want any breakfast. I'm too upset about Sal to eat," I said.

"You've got to come. Anyhow—your job is serving and cleaning duty this week," Carol reminded me. "Besides, not eating is not going to bring Sal back. It's probably better that he escaped."

"Better that he escaped? How could you say that, Carol?"

"Because an animal needs to be in its natural habitat. Sal probably wouldn't have lived very long in a container like that. Isn't it better for him to be out there in the woods where he's happy?"

I stared at her. "I never looked at it that way, Carol. Do you really think Sal is happier out there in the woods?"

"Absolutely." She put her hand on my shoulder. "Now how about washing your face and getting ready to join us in the dining room?"

Carol's words helped me pull myself together enough to join in the activities of the camp day. Still, there was this sense of unhappiness and loss that stayed with me. It got worse every time some kid came up to me to ask if he could hold Sal, and I had to say that Sal was gone. It got worse every time I looked at Brenda Roman and became more convinced she had to be the one who let Sal escape.

"There was no way Sal could have climbed up those steep smooth sides of plastic," I said to Farah later on that day. "It must have been Brenda who let him out, but I can't prove it."

95

"No more than you can prove she was the one who put Sal in your bed in the first place," said Farah. "Brenda's so sneaky. She knows how to pull things off without getting caught."

But Brenda didn't get away with the next sneaky thing she attempted to pull. It was at dinner that night, and Farah and I were bringing soup to the table. Brenda was sitting at the end near where we would have to pass in order to set our trays down on the serving cart.

I was busy keeping the soup steady so it wouldn't slosh out of the bowls. It was just plain luck that I happened to look down and notice that Brenda's pocketbook, which she liked to carry around with her, was sticking out in the aisle. As I approached, her foot pushed out the pocketbook, and I had to move to the side quickly to keep from tripping on it. I lost my balance and just barely managed to get my tray down on the cart without spilling anything.

It was only then that I remembered Farah was following closely behind me. She was carrying a tray with the remaining half-dozen bowls of soup. "Watch out for—" I began.

It was too late. Even as I spoke, Farah tripped over the pocketbook. Her feet went flying out from under her, and she landed on the floor, flat on her behind.

Farah tried to keep her grip on her tray, but that was an impossible task. The tray slipped from her grasp, and the bowls went crashing to the floor, splashing vegetable soup all over!

The crash was so loud that everyone in the dining room stood up to see what had caused it. Poor Farah's face screwed up, and I was sure she would start to cry. Then, above the questions of "What happened? What's going on?" a voice was heard.

"Look what you've done—you clumsy thing!" Brenda cried. "You've got soup all over my new pocketbook. You'll have to pay for it if it's ruined!"

I couldn't believe this, even coming from Brenda. There was poor Farah, struggling to get to her feet and clean off the soup that dripped from her body, and all Brenda could think of was her dumb pocketbook! There was no way I could keep silent now.

"Don't you say one more word about your precious pocketbook, Brenda! I saw you kick it out into the aisle to try to trip me. It's your fault Farah fell in the first place!"

"Brenda! Did you do that?" demanded Aileen as she dabbed Farah off with napkins from the table.

"Of course not," Brenda denied. "I wouldn't do anything to damage my own pocketbook, would I? It was Linda who knocked my pocketbook out into the aisle as she went by with her tray!"

I stared at her open-mouthed. I couldn't believe that even Brenda could lie so brazenly. And after doing such a terrible thing, too. Why, Farah could have been hurt, even burned if the soup had been hotter!

"Why you dirty, rotten liar—" I began.

"Let's not call anyone names here," Aileen interrupted me. "You're always quick to accuse Brenda of everything, Linda. I'm sure she would never do anything to try to hurt someone."

"That's right!" Brenda was smiling now that she saw Aileen was on her side, smiling her wicked, evil smile. "As usual, this was all Linda's fault."

"Liar!" I screamed, feeling hot anger rise to my head.

"Everyone knows that you're the liar, Linda," she calmly replied.

This accusation was what pushed me over the edge. I could no longer stand there, arguing with Brenda, trying to make Aileen or anyone else believe the truth about her. I had to find some way to make sure that Brenda wasn't going to get away with what she had done!

The bowls of soup were still sitting on the tray I had been carrying. Without thinking of the consequences, I grabbed a bowl and dumped it over Brenda's blow-dried head!"

Vegetable soup dripped down into her eyes and into her mouth. She let out a shriek that echoed through the dining room.

"What's going on here?" A horrified Mr. Hawkins ran over to our table.

"It's Linda, causing trouble again!" Aileen didn't hesitate before telling him.

"You should kick her out of camp right away," Brenda screamed. "Nobody wants her here, anyway!"

There was a moment of silence. I felt as if the eyes of everyone at camp were focused on me. I knew I was in big trouble now. What a disgrace it would be to wind up getting kicked out of camp.

"No one's going to kick me out of anywhere!" I said. "I'm leaving by myself!"

Before anyone could say or do anything to stop me, I had fled the dining room and was running across the field to the shelter of the woods.

Chapter
Thirteen

I didn't know where I was going. I didn't know what I was going to do. I only knew that I was burning up inside. I was furious at the evil thing Brenda had done and at her trying to blame me for it. I was angry at Aileen and Mr. Hawkins for taking Brenda's side. But what really upset me was the fact that just when I had come to really like Camp Winnepeg, this had to happen to ruin everything.

I had to get away. Away from the curious stares of the campers. Away from the condemning looks of the counselors. Away from the hateful, superior smile of Brenda Roman as she realized that, once again, she had gotten her way.

I was an outcast at camp, a known troublemaker. No one wanted me around, anyway. It was better that I went away and never saw anyone from Camp Winnepeg again.

With these thoughts echoing in my mind, I plunged

blindly into the woods. It occurred to me that I ought to go to my bunkhouse and get my jacket, a flashlight, and other things that would come in handy if I was out late at night, but I didn't dare. The bunkhouse was the first place anyone would look for me. There was no way I was going to let myself be caught.

Over bushes and under branches I went, my only thought to get away where no one could find me. But once I was what I figured was a safe distance away, I slowed down and began to think. It was late August, and the days were getting shorter now. It would be dark before long, and I had to decide what I was going to do. If I kept on heading blindly through the woods, I could wind up hopelessly lost.

I stopped and looked around me and listened for a moment. In the distance I could hear voices. I was sure it must be a group out to search for me and bring me back. What was I going to do?

In the distance I spotted a tree that looked good for climbing. Quickly I ran to it and swung up on the lowest bough. Then, as fast as I could, I climbed up high enough to be out of sight from the ground.

I made it up there just in time. Gasping for breath, I clung to a limb as the search party passed not twenty feet from the base of my tree.

"Linda? Where are you, Linda?" Mr. Hawkins called out. He was with Carol, Greg, and some of the other counselors. They searched the bushes, but none of them thought of looking up in the trees.

I said nothing. I waited until the search party was out of sight. Then I climbed down and looked around, trying to decide where to go.

I thought quickly. If camp was directly behind me, that meant the road that led into town was somewhere off to my left. If I could find that road, I could get to a place where there would be a phone so I could call my parents collect and have them come pick me up. It wouldn't be pleasant to face them, but it was better than having to go back to camp.

I started off in the direction I thought the road would be, but I soon stopped again. It was almost ten miles from camp to town. If I tried to get there tonight, I would be walking almost all that way in the dark. By the time I called my parents, it would be so late they would be frightened. And they'd be furious having to come get me in the middle of the night.

No, it would be better to wait until morning to go through the woods. For now I would build a lean-to and sleep in it overnight.

I walked on, looking for a place to build my lean-to. Soon I came to a clearing that looked about right. There were some large branches lying around that I could use for the frame and some smaller ones to put across it. I had no tools, so I would have to make do with what I could find.

I went right to work. Still, it was getting dark by the time I finished the lean-to. Dark and cold and damp. The air smelled humid. There were so many clouds in the sky, I couldn't see the stars. I sure hoped it wasn't going to rain.

I scooted under the lean-to and buried myself in the leaves I had piled on the bottom. They did nothing to keep me warm. And the rocks underneath poked into my back every way I turned.

How I wished I had a fire. How I wished this terrible night would end and I was back safely home again.

I couldn't fall asleep. Somewhere, in the distance, I heard howling. I heard it again, closer this time. A shiver of fear went up my spine.

My heart was pounding. I sat up in the lean-to and peered outside. Shadows moved in the nearby bushes. What if it was a wild animal?

"You're being silly!" I said to myself. The chances of coming across a wild animal so close to camp were very small. I sat there, breathing deeply and trying to calm myself down. I had almost succeeded when I saw a flash of lightening and heard a clap of thunder. Those clouds blocking the stars were storm clouds. I had to find a better shelter. My makeshift lean-to would never protect me from lightening or a heavy rain.

I had no choice but to head back toward camp. It was very slow moving through the woods in the dark. I wasn't even sure I was going in the right direction until I managed to catch sight of a light glimmering in the distance. Lightening flashed, followed by thunder, closer this time. The wind picked up and began to howl. The storm was almost upon me. I went faster, hoping to find someplace to hide before the rain hit.

I didn't make it. It was pouring by the time I reached the campgrounds. Rain slashed against my face and soaked my clothing. I couldn't go on any farther. I raced for the first building I came to and dashed up the steps to the porch.

I was in luck. There was a big overhang that was enough to keep the rain off me. And there was some porch furniture. I saw a rattan sofa where I thought I might be able to sleep the night.

I was so grateful to be out of the rain that it took me a moment to realize that this was no ordinary camp bunkhouse porch. Ordinary camp bunks didn't have rattan porch furniture. There was an opening in the drapes that covered the window, and I tiptoed over to peek inside. What I saw was a living room, filled with flower-print sofas and chairs and lit by a roaring fire. And there was Mr. Hawkins. He must have just come back from searching for me because he was peeling off his wet jacket and warming himself by the fire. His wife came in and gave him a towel. He used it to dry his face and hair.

I couldn't believe it! Of all the places to pick to take shelter, I had to wind up at the Hawkins's home! I thought of making a run for another building but decided against it. It was raining too hard now, and there was nothing close enough. I was already too wet and too cold.

Besides, when I thought about it, maybe it wasn't so terrible to be on the Hawkins's porch. It was the last place anyone would think of looking for me, and from here I could keep track of what was going on around camp. I pressed myself up against the window, hoping to feel some warmth filtering through from inside. That's when I realized that if I put my ear right up against the glass, I could hear what Mr. Hawkins was saying.

"What a terrible night! We searched the entire area close to camp, but we weren't able to find her. I had to call everyone back once the storm had started. After all, the counselors are just college students, and I'm responsible for them, too. But I can't let a ten-year-old stay out in the woods in a storm at night. It's time to get help from professionals. I'm going to have to call her parents and the police."

My parents! The police! I was horrified. I hadn't thought that Mr. Hawkins might call my parents. I certainly hadn't thought that he might call in the police. I couldn't allow that to happen. My parents would be so worried, thinking I was lost out there in a rainstorm in the woods. The police would be furious to find out that I really wasn't.

Not only that, I was so cold now that I was shivering. I could get really sick if I were to stay outside any longer.

There was only one thing for me to do now. I had to turn myself in to Mr. Hawkins and face the consequences.

Chapter
Fourteen

My heart was hammering as I knocked at the thick wooden door and waited for it to open. I braced myself for the anger and rage I would soon receive from Mr. Hawkins.

Mrs. Hawkins was the one who answered the door. "Linda? Is that you?" she gasped.

"Y-yes," I admitted unhappily.

"Thank goodness!" Her face actually lit up. "Bruce, don't call anyone yet. It's Linda! She's here at our door!"

Mr. Hawkins came rushing over. I waited to receive the harsh words and punishment I knew I deserved.

But to my surprise, the only emotion Mr. Hawkins showed was concern. "Come in the house right away, Linda," he ordered. He put his arm around my shoulder. "You're all wet and you're shivering. We've got to get you out of those wet clothes. Diane, bring Linda a robe to put on, please. I'll notify everyone she's been found and then make us all something hot to drink. Do you like hot chocolate, Linda?"

"Uh-huh." I nodded, overwhelmed by all this attention. I stretched my hands out toward the fire to warm them. The heat felt wonderful. It was almost worth facing Mr. Hawkins to be able to feel warm again.

It wasn't until I was wrapped in the robe and seated in the comfortable chair in front of the fire with my hot chocolate in hand that Mr. Hawkins got down to business.

"Linda, I don't know if you have any idea of how worried everyone was about you. It was a terrible thing for you to go running off into the woods that way. Anything could have happened to you. You might have been lost or seriously hurt or even killed. The entire camp was upset because you had disappeared. Half the staff was out there in the woods tonight searching for you. They didn't come back until it started to storm.

"I know," I admitted. "I saw your group go by."

"You saw our group go by and you didn't say anything? Why on earth not? Didn't you know how worried we would be?"

"No, I didn't," I said quietly. "I thought everyone from camp was angry at me and never wanted to see me again. I knew everyone blamed me for that scene in the dining room. I'm always blamed for everything with Brenda. Everyone thinks that she's so wonderful and I'm nothing but a troublemaker. A tomboy terror or something!"

"A tomboy terror?" Mr. Hawkins let out a laugh. "Well, I guess there have been moments when you

107

could have been described that way, Linda, but this isn't one of them. You see, no one's blaming you for what happened."

"They're not?" I couldn't believe it. "How come?"

"Because this time there were witnesses to that little scene. Greg, the boys' counselor, was on his way to your table to talk to Aileen as you went by with your tray. He saw everything."

I gasped. "Everything?"

"That's right, everything. He told us that Brenda kicked her pocketbook out into the aisle as you came by. He described how you narrowly missed tripping on it and how Farah did trip on it and fell. He told us how Brenda tried to make it look as if it were your fault."

"Wow!" I was overwhelmed by this news. Brenda had been found guilty without my having to do a thing. "I hope you're going to give Brenda the punishment she deserves," I said. In my mind I pictured her up on the stage, wearing a sign that said Liar in big letters around her neck. Everyone in camp was pointing at her and laughing. It was wonderful to think about it.

"I had a private discussion with Brenda about what she did," Mr. Hawkins said. "She understands that it was wrong, and I'm sure nothing like that will happen again."

"A private discussion with Brenda? Big deal! That's typical of her to get off with no punishment at all. She always has everything go exactly her way!"

"That's not true," Mr. Hawkins replied. "Brenda is actually a very sad little girl."

108

"Brenda? Sad? What do you mean, Mr. Hawkins? Brenda has everything she could possibly want!"

"Not really, Linda. You live in her apartment building in the city. I'm sure you're aware that Brenda is alone most of the time. Her parents are very busy with the business they own. They work long hours and have little time for her. Brenda has no brothers and sisters and not many friends. Think about that."

I tried, but I was way too tired to do much thinking. Especially about Brenda. I stifled a yawn. Suddenly exhaustion caught up with me.

Mr. Hawkins saw this and stood up from his seat. "But that's enough talk about Brenda for now. It's late, and you need to get some sleep. Suppose we put you in our guest room for tonight? It's a lot warmer there than in your bunkhouse, and we can keep an eye on you to make sure you're not coming down with anything."

"Fine with me," I said, yawning again.

The quilt and pillows on the guest room bed were thick, warm, and comfortable. I wondered briefly how the experiences of tonight were going to change things for me at camp. But before I could give any thought to the situation, I was fast asleep.

Chapter
Fifteen

I woke up with the morning sun on my face. It took me a while to realize where I was. And then I remembered all that had happened yesterday. I was in the Hawkins's guest room.

The bed was so comfortable that I didn't want to get up. But then I heard knocking at the door. "Come in," I said.

Mrs. Hawkins stuck her head in the room. "I hate to wake you, Linda, but I don't want you to miss breakfast. If you hurry, you can still catch your bunk in the dining room. I did some laundry this morning. Here are your clothes, clean and dry and ready for you to wear."

"Thanks," I said gratefully. I still couldn't get over how nice Mr. and Mrs. Hawkins had been to me. I felt awful for having caused them so much trouble. And I felt very uncomfortable at the thought of having to face the kids in my bunk after all that had happened.

To my surprise, with the exception of Brenda, of course, the girls in my bunk treated me almost as if I were some sort of returning hero. They crowded around me, throwing questions at me.

"How scary was it to be out alone in the woods at night, Linda?" "How did you manage to get through the storm?" "Weren't you afraid of all that thunder and lightening?" "How did you escape without being found?" "What was it like inside the Hawkins's house?" "What did they do to you when you turned yourself in?"

I was so busy trying to answer these questions that it took me a while to realize that Sharon and Melissa were part of the group that was gathered around me. Brenda was sitting alone on her bed. She was trying to look as if she were fascinated with a book that was open on her lap, but I could tell by her face that she felt sad and left out.

Aileen went over to Brenda and gave her a nudge. "Why don't you go over to Linda and tell her what you have to say right now, Brenda?" Aileen said.

All color drained from Brenda's face. She forced herself up from her bed and slowly walked over to where I was standing.

The kids in the bunk dropped back to clear a path for her. Everyone waited to see what would happen between us.

"I—uh—I want to a-pol—apologize." Brenda practically choked on the word. "I did try to trip you yesterday, and I'm sorry that Farah fell and that I—uh—I tried to blame you!"

I stood there, listening to Brenda and watching her

111

discomfort. I could imagine the pressure that must have been put on her to get her to make this apology to me. Whatever it was, the result was that I had her now. Here she was, apologizing to me in front of the entire bunk. This was the perfect opportunity for me to give her what she deserved, to say something that would embarrass her so badly that she could never face anyone again.

But as I struggled to come up with a nasty enough remark, I looked at Brenda's face. She looked so sad and alone I almost felt sorry for her.

Why, Mr. Hawkins was right, I realized suddenly. Brenda is an unhappy person. Not only that, but she's her own worst enemy. She wants friends, but the way she acts keeps them away from her. She winds up punishing herself.

When I realized this, it was as if a tremendous weight was lifted from my shoulders. There really was no reason for me to have to "get" Brenda or embarrass her. "Aw, forget it, Brenda," I said before I even knew the words were coming. "There are only a few days left of camp now, anyway. It shouldn't be so hard for us to get along."

I wish I could say that I came to like Brenda in those last days of camp, but I still found her totally obnoxious. I wish I could say that I didn't feel a stab of jealousy when she announced that her parents had notified her they had bought a new home which they would be moving to in time for the new school year. Unfortunately, it still made me sick to think that stuck-up Brenda was going to live in a big, beautiful house while I was returning to my way-too-small New York City apartment.

But this time my jealous feelings didn't last too long. Even as Brenda went on and on about how lucky she was to be moving to this wonderful neighborhood and to be able to fix up her new room any way she wanted it, I remembered what Mr. Hawkins had told me about how unhappy she was inside. Brenda's new house would be as empty as her old apartment had been. Brenda would be just as sad and lonely unless she made some big changes. I actually felt sorry for Brenda. It must be awful when all you had were material things.

The last night of camp we had a tremendous campfire. Mr. and Mrs. Hawkins were right up there with the camp cook and the counselors, handing out hotdogs and beans to everyone.

After we cleaned up, we sat around the fire in groups and sang camp songs. Then Mr. Hawkins began the big event of the evening—giving out awards to the campers for our accomplishments this summer. Mr. Hawkins called a kid's name and read out what the award was for. Everyone cheered while he or she came up for the award.

It must have been pretty difficult to come up with an award for everyone, but the counselors managed to do it. Some of the awards were pretty silly, like the one to Brad for having the most perfectly clean plates at meals. Some were meaningless, like the one to Brenda

113

for being the best-dressed camper. But some of them really meant a lot, like the one to Farah for showing the most improvement in swimming.

"This should really go to you, Linda," Farah beamed as she showed her printed award paper to me.

I only had time to smile at her before I heard my own name being called. "Linda Berman, to whom I want to give special recognition for uniting boys' and girls' sports at Camp Winnepeg," Mr. Hawkins's voice rang out. "Thanks, Linda."

There were lots of cheers at that and a few boos from the people who still thought that boys' and girls' sports should be separate. Mr. Hawkins held out a hand to quiet everyone down. "Here's your award, Linda, for being the Most Tamed Tomboy Terror Camp Winnepeg has ever known!"

Everyone burst out laughing at this announcement, and I couldn't help but laugh myself. I guess I could see why I might have been thought of as a "Tomboy Terror" at the beginning of camp. I was sure glad to be ending it on a more peaceful note.

"Hey, Linda," Brad called out to me as I returned to my seat in the circle. "I noticed your hair has grown so much you're starting to look like a girl. Sam just said he's available to give you a haircut before we go back home again!"

I looked at Sam and Brad and Matt, who were sitting there grinning at me. I really liked those guys—I would have had a great time being in their bunk this summer, if I had gotten away with my scheme.

But then I looked at Farah, and Rachel and Heather, and the other girls in my bunk, and realized I had had a great time with them as well. Especially now that I had learned not to let Brenda Roman get to me.

"No, thanks." I grinned back at the boys happily. "I think I'll start this school year as a girl!"

Awards were over. Everyone joined hands with the kids sitting next to them, and we ended the campfire with our camp song.

Here's to you, our Camp Winnepeg.
We salute you with our song.
Swimming, hiking, art, and sports,
It's fun the whole day long.
But the things we hold most dear
Are the friendships we make that last all year.
We can't wait to come back here
And be together again, singing:
Here's to you, our Camp Winnepeg.
We salute you with our song!

I couldn't believe it. My eyes were actually filled with tears at the thought of leaving Camp Winnepeg and the friends I had made. Even Brenda!

It had turned out to be a wonderful summer after all!

To find out what happened
to Linda in fifth grade,
read *2 Young 2 Go 4 Boys*.

About the Author

LINDA LEWIS was graduated from City College of New York and received her master's degree in special education. She has written seven Archway Paperbacks about Linda in the following sequence: *We Hate Everything but Boys, Is There Life After Boys?, We Love Only Older Boys, My Heart Belongs to That Boy, All for the Love of That Boy, Dedicated to That Boy I Love,* and *Loving Two Is Hard to Do.* She has also written three books about Linda for younger readers, *Want to Trade Two Brothers for a Cat?, The Tomboy Terror in Bunk 109,* and *2 Young 2 Go 4 Boys,* which are available from Minstrel Books. Ms. Lewis now resides in Lauderdale-by-the-Sea, Florida. She is married and has two children.

Printed in the United States
By Bookmasters